STUDENT DRAMA SERIES

General Editor: MICHAEL MARLAND, B.A.

A
KIND
OF
LOVING

TITLES IN THE SERIES

A
KIND
OF
LOVING

BY STAN BARSTOW
and
ALFRED BRADLEY

BASED ON THE NOVEL BY Stan Barstow

EDITED BY MICHAEL MARLAND, B.A.

With a note by Alfred Bradley

BLACKIE *LONDON & GLASGOW*

Blackie & Son Limited
BISHOPBRIGGS, GLASGOW G64 2NZ
FURNIVAL HOUSE, 14–18 HIGH HOLBORN,
LONDON WCIV 6BX

A Kind of Loving   ©   *Stan Barstow and Alfred Bradley 1970*
Notes and Questions   ©   *Michael Marland 1970*
Novel into Play   ©   *Blackie and Son Limited 1970*

FIRST PUBLISHED 1970
0 216 87634 6

PRINTED IN GREAT BRITAIN BY
WESTERN PRINTING SERVICES LTD, BRISTOL

CONTENTS

ACKNOWLEDGMENTS

The editor is grateful to the following, for their help in the preparation of this volume:

Mr. Stan Barstow and Mr. Alfred Bradley for *A Kind of Loving*.
Mr. Alfred Bradley for the article, *Novel into Play*.
Sheffield Playhouse and Mr. Edward Furby for the ground plan and scene settings from the Sheffield Production.
York Theatre Royal and the Press Agency (Yorkshire) Limited for the photographs from the York Production.
Anglo Amalgamated Film Distributors Limited for stills from the film.

A Kind of Loving

by Stan Barstow
and Alfred Bradley

The play takes place in a small Yorkshire mining town. The individual scenes flow into one another without a break, except for the fading down of the lights on one set, and up on another. The various places in which the scenes take place can be very simply indicated, and the stage can be set for various scenes at the same time.

THE CHARACTERS

VIC BROWN
ARTHUR BROWN, his father
MRS. BROWN, his mother
AUNT EDNA
CHRISTINE, his sister

CONROY
WILLY
RAWLINSON
HASSOP
} draughtsmen who work with Vic

INGRID ROTHWELL
MR. ROTHWELL, her father
MRS. ROTHWELL, her mother
DOROTHY, a friend of Ingrid's

MR. VAN HUYTEN
A GIRL CUSTOMER
A MAN CUSTOMER
} in Mr. Van Huyten's record shop

MRS. OLIPHANT, a neighbour
DR. PARKER, a woman doctor

Act 1

SCENE I   THE BROWNS' LIVING-ROOM
It is Boxing Day and Christine's wedding morning.

MRS. BROWN *is doing her hair in the mirror over the fireplace. During the scene she will also put on her hat. These operations impede her husband,* ARTHUR, *who is having trouble with a new shirt and tie and can't get to the mirror to see what he's doing.*

1   MRS. BROWN. Have you seen our Victor, lately?

2   ARTHUR. He's not far away.

3   MRS. BROWN [*calls*]. Victor! Victor, are you ready?

> VIC BROWN *enters. He wears a dark grey lounge suit and is carrying his jacket. He feels in the pockets and produces a piece of paper.*

4   VIC. Are you shouting, Mother?

5   MRS. BROWN. Yes. Are you ready?

6   VIC. All about.

7   MRS. BROWN. Well don't hang about. You know we haven't a lot of time this morning.

8   VIC. You're telling me.

9   MRS. BROWN. And have you got them taxis worked out properly?

10 VIC. I know it all by heart. [*flourishes piece of paper*] The first car picks up Uncle Edward and Auntie Eileen and deposits at church. From church proceed to Cousin Clifford's, pick him up with Cousin Mary and little Angela, call at Moorside Road on return journey and collect Mr. and Mrs. Humbleby and deposit at church. *They'll* all have a longish wait. Meanwhile, the other car proceeds . . .

> MRS. BROWN *turns from mirror and* ARTHUR *takes his chance.*

1   MRS. BROWN. All right, all right. There's no need to make it into a recitation. As long as you know what you're doing.

2   ARTHUR. You haven't forgotten your sister, have you?

3   VIC. That'd be a fine thing, wouldn't it? Get everybody there but the bride.

4   MRS. BROWN. You just see that you do get her there. And on time.

   MRS. BROWN *exits into kitchen.*

5   ARTHUR. Well thank the Lord I've only got one daughter. I wouldn't want to go through all this again. When it's your turn, lad, I'll be able to sit back and watch some other poor beggar footing the bill.

6   VIC. That'll be the day!

   ARTHUR *carries on struggling with his collar and* VIC *becomes preoccupied with his schedule as* AUNT EDNA *bustles in and looks quickly round the room at floor level.*

7   EDNA. Well, I don't know . . .

8   ARTHUR. What you rootin' about at, Edna?

9   EDNA. Me other shoe. You haven't seen it, have you?

10 ARTHUR [*preoccupied*]. What's it look like?

11 EDNA. Like this one I've got on.

   VIC *comes out of his list for a minute.*

12 VIC. What's up, Auntie?

13 EDNA. I put both me shoes down under the table last night and this morning I could only find one.

14 VIC. There was our Lily's little lad playing with summat in the garden.

15 EDNA. Oh, the little devil! He's into everything.

   EDNA *steps out of other shoe, leaving it behind as she rushes through doorway into hall.* VIC *picks up the shoe and puts it on the table.* MRS. BROWN *comes in from kitchen, lightly brushing herself down with her hands.*

2

1 MRS. BROWN. There, I've put the kettle on for a cup of tea. Who's put that shoe on the table? Don't you know it's bad luck?

2 VIC [*moving shoe*]. Only if there's a 'y' in the month.

3 MRS. BROWN. Don't talk so daft. What you hanging about here for, anyway?

4 VIC. I can't do anything till the first car comes.

5 MRS. BROWN. Well, keep one eye out for it, and just give your father a hand or else he won't be ready for Easter.

ARTHUR *pulls at his collar.*

6 ARTHUR. I can never get knot right with a new tie.

7 VIC. Here, let's look.

VIC *pulls at the tie.*

8 ARTHUR. Ho'd on, don't strangle me.

9 VIC. You want to look smart, don't you?

10 ARTHUR. I want to get me breath an' all.

11 VIC. There you are. That'll do.

ARTHUR *stretches his neck.*

12 ARTHUR. It won't be for long, I suppose.

13 VIC. Where did you get the tie?

14 ARTHUR. Our Christine bought it for me.

15 VIC. I thought it was a bit 'with it' for you.

16 ARTHUR. I wish this suit was a bit more with it.

17 VIC. What's up with it? I think he's made a right good job of it.

18 ARTHUR. I just don't feel right in it, some road.

19 VIC. But he's one of the best tailors in Cressley, Dad.

20 ARTHUR. I knew he must be when he told me t'price. All t'same I wish I'd gone to Liversidge's like I allus do.

21 VIC. Ah, they cut clothes with a bacon slicer there. That'll be a suit when you've forgotten how much you paid for it. And that's looking a long time ahead.

EDNA *comes in with the other shoe.*

3

1 EDNA. Now where have they put the other . . . [VIC *hands her the shoe she left behind.*] Oh, thank you Victor. [*She holds up the shoes.*] Just look at this one. He's had the toe in his mouth and sucked all the shine off.

2 MRS. BROWN. Eeh, Edna, you allus did need an army to wait on you. Come on in here an' I'll give you some polish.

3 VIC [*teasing*]. And keep an eye out for that taxi.

MRS. BROWN and EDNA go into kitchen.

4 ARTHUR. It's not time yet, surely.

5 VIC. You've got plenty of time.

A brass band outside begins to play Hark, the Herald Angels.

6 ARTHUR. Listen, here's t'band. They said they'd call round. [*They listen.*] How d'you think they sound?

7 VIC. They sound all right to me.

8 ARTHUR. I haven't missed a Boxing Day play-out in years.

9 VIC [*wickedly*]. They seem to be managing without you.

10 ARTHUR. I'll just go and have a word with 'em.

MRS BROWN pops her head round kitchen door.

11 MRS. BROWN. Don't you go inviting that lot to have drinks this morning, Arthur. We haven't time to be bothered with them today.

12 ARTHUR. All right, all right.

He goes to hall door and opens it as CHRISTINE *appears, in dressing-gown.*

13 CHRISTINE. Oh, hello, Dad. I see the band's come to serenade me.

14 ARTHUR. Aye, I'm just going to have a word with 'em. [*He goes out.*]

15 VIC [*calls after him*]. You've forgotten your trombone, Dad. [*grins at* CHRIS] Anybody'd think it was him getting married.

16 CHRISTINE. I'm beginning to wish it was somebody else.

[*She takes box from top of sideboard, opens it and takes out bridal headdress and veil.*]

1 VIC. Got cold feet, have you, love?

2 CHRISTINE. I'll just be glad when it's all over. I feel it's got nothing to do with me any more.

3 VIC. Aye, it turns into a feast day for the relatives. Registry office for me.

4 CHRISTINE. Oh? Have you got somebody in mind?

5 VIC. Well, there is somebody I'm a bit interested in. But I've hardly spoken to her yet so don't you go giving me mother ideas.

MRS. BROWN *comes in from kitchen.*

6 MRS. BROWN. Honestly, I'll be glad when it's . . . [*She stops short on seeing* CHRISTINE.] Aren't you dressed yet?

7 CHRISTINE. I'm all ready underneath. I've just my dress to slip on.

8 MRS. BROWN. What about them bridesmaids' bouquets?

9 CHRISTINE. It's all taken care of.

EDNA *comes in with two cups of tea.*

10 EDNA. Here, Lucy, sit down and have a cup of tea. You'll be worn out before you ever get to the church.

11 MRS. BROWN. How can I sit down when our Christine isn't even dressed yet?

12 CHRISTINE. Oh, look, I'll go and get dressed now.

13 MRS. BROWN. I'll come with you.

14 EDNA. You'll drink this cup of tea and stay where you are for a minute.

15 CHRISTINE. Yes, you keep her quiet, Auntie Edna. I'll give you a shout when I need you.

CHRISTINE *goes out as* ARTHUR *comes back in.*

16 ARTHUR. You're not going down the aisle like that, are you? Isn't it—

17 CHRISTINE [*finishes it for him*]. Yes, time I was dressed. [*She goes.*]

5

1 EDNA. There's a cup of tea in the kitchen, Arthur.

2 ARTHUR. I need summat stronger than tea this morning.

   ARTHUR *goes into kitchen and returns during next conversation.* VIC *stands at window and alternately peers down the road and consults his list.*

3 EDNA. You'll miss her, Lucy.

4 MRS. BROWN. Aye, she's a good lass, our Christine. But it's high time she settled down and started a family. Many a lass at twenty-seven has 'em growing up and going to school.

5 EDNA. I must say David seems a right nice young man.

6 MRS. BROWN. Oh, he is. A grand lad.

7 EDNA. So nicely spoken, and such lovely manners.

8 ARTHUR. He's educated, David is. Educated.

9 MRS. BROWN. She'll be all right with him. We haven't a minute's worry about that.

10 EDNA. I think you've both got plenty to be proud of—a daughter a teacher and a son a draughtsman ...

11 ARTHUR. A collier can do summat for his bairns nowadays, Edna.

12 EDNA. It'll be Victor's turn next, I suppose.

   VIC *half turns his head at this.*

13 MRS. BROWN. Oh, we shan't be going to our Victor's wedding yet a while. Give him time. He's hardly twenty-one, and he's not courting as far as I know.

14 EDNA. Young men don't tell their mothers everything, y'know, Lucy.

15 VIC. Catch me on this caper.

16 MRS. BROWN. One of 'em will catch you one o' these fine days.

17 VIC. She'll have to be up early.

   A taxi horn honks outside.

18 MRS. BROWN. There's that taxi now. [VIC *crosses to mantelpiece and takes a key.*] Now what are you after?

1 VIC. Just the key in case I forget.

2 MRS. BROWN. What do you want that for?

3 VIC. There's a dance on in town. I thought I'd pop over tonight.

4 MRS. BROWN. Well don't be thinking about that. You see 'at all them people get to church. And don't be coming in late. You'll be on the go all day and you've got to be back at work tomorrow. Don't forget.

5 VIC. Don't worry, I won't forget.

He goes out as lights fade on the scene and come up on the Drawing Office.

SCENE 2   THE DRAWING OFFICE AT DAWSON WHITTAKER'S
             Late afternoon

VIC, CONROY, WILLY, RAWLINSON. They are all in their early twenties except CONROY who is a little older and more experienced than the others. They work at separate boards. The lighting should be able to suggest a separate light over each board so that when VIC is left alone in the office he is working in just the one light with shadows round him.
CONROY straightens up.

6 CONROY. That's that. [*He tidies the drawings on his board and goes over to get his coat which he brings and throws over his stool for a moment.*]

7 WILLY. Number one trap tonight, Conroy.

8 CONROY. They've had their money's worth off me today and there's no point in starting anything else. [*turns to tease* RAWLY] Nearly time to go home to Mummy.

9 RAWLY. What? [*with no trace of humour*] I only make it twenty-five past.

10 CONROY. Oh, sorry I interrupted you.

11 RAWLY. We're paid to work till half-past, aren't we?

12 CONROY. You're so right. Where would Whittaker's be if everybody knocked off early? [*He wanders round to* WILLY's

place and picks a book of pin-ups off the board.] Hmmm, somebody studying isometrics.

2 WILLY. Aye, there's some beautiful detailing in there. Look at that one! What a body! It makes you feel badly.

3 VIC. Where did you get it, Willy?

4 WILLY. A mate of mine brought it back from Paris. That's where I'm going for me holidays next year.

5 VIC. He thinks they walk about the streets with nothing on.

6 WILLY. No, but there's plenty of it waiting for you. And you don't have to look far for it. *[He wriggles his hips.]* Cherchez la femme.

7 CONROY. You're a bloke who'll get summat he won't get rid of so quick.

8 WILLY. Ah, science, man, science.

9 CONROY. What does a bird on a street corner know about science?

10 VIC. Watch it!

WILLY *whips the book out of sight as* HASSOP *walks in.*

11 HASSOP. What's this, then, a Mothers' Meeting? You, Brown, you know that Wellington job's needed by Wednesday morning.

12 VIC. It'll be ready, Mr. Hassop.

13 HASSOP. I'd feel happier if you'd put in a bit of overtime on it tonight. There's that extension job as well. They'll be screaming for that soon.

14 VIC. I'll stay on for a while then, if you like.

HASSOP *nods and begins to go off other side, to his own office. He speaks to* CONROY *as he passes.*

15 HASSOP. I wasn't aware that it was half-past five, Conroy.

16 CONROY. It is by my watch. *[as* HASSOP *goes]* Why didn't you tell him to get stuffed?

17 VIC. Well, he's right. I knew all along when it was wanted.

18 CONROY. Fair enough. If you can't get your work done in office hours you've got to work over.

1 VIC [*good-humoured*]. Ah, get on with you, bighead.

The finishing bell rings, and CONROY *picks up a tin lid and bangs it with a ruler near* RAWLY's *ear.*

2 CONROY. Five-thirty, thou good and faithful servant. [*They are all putting their coats on except* VIC *and* RAWLY.] Goodnight to you, brother.

3 VIC. 'Night.

4 CONROY. Do us a nice picture of Hassop's extension. [*He goes out.*]

5 WILLY. So long, Vic.

6 VIC. 'Night, Willy.

WILLY goes out. RAWLY *fusses for a minute, then follows.*

7 RAWLY. Goodnight.

8 VIC. 'Night. [RAWLY *carefully switches off all the lights, including* VIC's, *by mistake.* VIC *shouts good-naturedly.*] Hey up!

RAWLY puts VIC's *light back on.*

9 RAWLY. Sorry. [*goes out*]

VIC *settles down to his work and there is a pause before the door opens suddenly and* INGRID *comes in, carrying a small parcel.*

10 INGRID. Oh, I thought everybody had gone.

VIC *is surprised and delighted to see her.*

11 VIC. Hello. Did you want something?

12 INGRID. You caught me in the act. I was sneaking in to borrow a pencil.

13 VIC. A pencil?

14 INGRID. Well, a blue crayon, really. I've got to register this parcel and the post-room's closed. I shall have to pop it in at the general on my way home.

15 VIC. I think we can fix you up. [*Gets blue pencil.*] Oh, hang on. [*He puts point on pencil with his knife.*] Funny how people find rush jobs when you're ready to finish.

16 INGRID. You've got one, too, have you? Mine doesn't think of starting his letters till it's nearly time to go. It's Miss

9

Rothwell this and Miss Rothwell that in office hours, but after time it's 'I say, Ingrid, would you mind just doing this for me?'

2 VIC. Here we are. [*hands her pencil*]

3 INGRID. Thank you. [*starts to mark up parcel*]

4 VIC. Would you like me to drop it in for you? I go that way.

5 INGRID. It's all right, thanks. I have to pass the door.

6 VIC. If you can hang on a minute, I'll walk down with you.

7 INGRID. I thought you were working over.

8 VIC. I've more or less finished. It'll do tomorrow.

9 INGRID. All right, then. [*She sticks stamps and label on parcel as* VIC *clears his board.*] That was your sister's wedding at St. Mark's on Boxing Day, wasn't it?

10 VIC. Yes, our Chris. Did you see it?

11 INGRID. I was just passing when they came out so I stopped to watch. I love weddings.

12 VIC. We shall be getting the photos before long. I could bring them in for you to see, if you like.

13 INGRID. Yes, I'd like to look at them.

A pause.

14 VIC. It's funny, isn't it?

15 INGRID. What?

16 VIC. I've seen you about a lot but this is the first time we've really talked to each other.

17 INGRID. Yes, it is funny.

VIC *clears his throat.*

18 VIC. Look, I was wondering . . .

INGRID *starts to speak before he's finished.*

19 INGRID. I suppose it happens with a lot of . . . I'm sorry, what were you saying?

20 VIC. Oh, it was nothing.

21 INGRID. Don't be silly. Go on.

1 VIC. I was wondering if we might, you know, some night when you're not busy . . .

2 INGRID [*helping him to say it*]. They say that Doris Day picture at the Palace is good.

3 VIC. What about seeing it together?

4 INGRID. When would you want to go?

5 VIC. Any time. Tomorrow would suit me.

6 INGRID. I can't tomorrow. What about Wednesday?

7 VIC. Yes, fine, Wednesday. I'll meet you outside. What time does it start?

8 INGRID. I'm not sure, but we can have a look on the way down town now.

9 VIC. Yes, right.

10 INGRID. Ready?

11 VIC. Yes, ready.

He holds the door open for her to go out, then he comes back with a very happy smile on his face and switches off the last light.

SCENE 3   THE BROWNS' LIVING-ROOM
Evening

ARTHUR *sits in a chair, fiddling with his trombone. He blows through the instrument without making a sound and then dismantles it and cleans it with a piece of rag. This business goes on through the scene.* VIC *comes in in shirt-sleeves.*

12 VIC. Are you going to practise?

13 ARTHUR. I thought I'd have half an hour to keep me lip in while your mother's out.

14 VIC. I say, Dad.

15 ARTHUR. What's up?

16 VIC. You know that tie our Chris bought you for the wedding? Can I borrow it?

17 ARTHUR. It's in me drawer . . . You've enough ties to stretch from here to Huddersfield and back.

VIC *takes the tie from a sideboard drawer, unrolls it and holds it up.*

1 VIC. This is nice, though.

2 ARTHUR. One tie's as good as another to me.

3 VIC. You might as well give me this one, then.

4 ARTHUR. Nay, I shall have to wear it when we go round to our Christine's next week. I don't want to offend her.

5 VIC. I can borrow it, though?

6 ARTHUR. You could borrow that suit if it'd fit you.

   VIC *is putting on the tie.*

7 VIC. Now don't start all that again.

8 ARTHUR. I've never felt so tethered up in all me life.

9 VIC. Look, there's nothing wrong with this suit, is there?

   ARTHUR *glances dispassionately at* VIC.

10 ARTHUR. It's all right for a young feller.

11 VIC [*disgusted*]. Aagh!

12 ARTHUR. What you getting all dolled up for, any road?

13 VIC. I'm going out.

14 ARTHUR. I didn't think you were going to bed. Is it summat special?

15 VIC. Why should it be special?

16 ARTHUR [*to himself*]. Mind your own business, lad. Mind your own business.

   VIC *is fingering his chin in the mirror.*

17 VIC. Do you think I need a shave?

18 ARTHUR. I've seen better whiskers on cheese.

19 VIC. Go on. Have you got the right time? My watch is playing up.

20 ARTHUR. Twenty past.

21 VIC. Is it? I thought it was only just turned seven.

   He dashes about, getting his coat.

22 ARTHUR. What's up, won't she wait for you?

23 VIC. Who?

1 ARTHUR [*sardonically*]. Who? Brigitte flippin' Bardot, o' course.

> VIC *is at the door.*

2 VIC. You can tell me mam I won't be late.

> *He goes out.* ARTHUR, *his trombone reassembled, blows a note that comes out like a raspberry. He looks at the instrument with some surprise.*

SCENE 4   THE PARK
Night

VIC *and* INGRID *are strolling home.*

3 INGRID. He's had this job for a long time. He's a site engineer for a big construction firm and he goes all over the country on different jobs. Even abroad sometimes. [*She stumbles.*] Oh!

> VIC *takes her arm.*

4 VIC. Are you all right?

5 INGRID. Yes, I think so. [*She rubs her ankle.*]

6 VIC. Here, sit down here for a minute.

> *He leads her to a bench and she sits down.*

7 INGRID. I'm all right. I just went over on my ankle.

8 VIC. You were saying . . .

9 INGRID. Yes, about Daddy.

10 VIC. It must be like being married to a sailor.

11 INGRID. That's just what Mother says. But they're very affectionate when he is at home so I suppose that helps to make up for it. Not that Mother seems to mind being separated a lot most of the time. 'Course, it'll be lonelier for her when she hasn't got me for company.

> VIC *joins her on the bench.*

12 VIC. Are you thinking of leaving home, then?

13

1 INGRID. I suppose I shall one day. When I get married, I mean.

2 VIC. How old are you, Ingrid?

3 INGRID. Eighteen, nearly nineteen.

4 VIC. You're only a kid.

5 INGRID. Hark at Father Time!

6 VIC. And what sort of bloke are you going to marry, then?

7 INGRID. Well *I* don't want to be a sailor's wife. I want somebody who'll be with me all the time.

8 VIC. You'll have to wait and see who turns up.

9 INGRID. How do you know he hasn't turned up already?

10 VIC. What are you doing out with me, then?

11 INGRID. Making him jealous!

12 VIC. Is he a big bloke?

13 INGRID. Big enough.

VIC *pretends to raise his hat and leave her.*

14 VIC. I'll say goodnight, then.

15 INGRID [*laughing*]. Don't worry, I'll protect you.

16 VIC. I'm sorry I kept you waiting tonight.

17 INGRID. You don't have to keep on apologizing. I knew you'd come.

18 VIC. I'm not usually late. I don't know what's happened to this watch.

19 INGRID. As long as you're not disappointed now.

20 VIC. No. [*a pause*] Did you like the picture?

21 INGRID. Loved it. Didn't you?

22 VIC. It was all right, I suppose. A bit thin, I thought.

23 INGRID. I just go to be entertained.

24 VIC. Well, so do I, but I like a picture with a bit of something about it.

25 INGRID. You should have said. We could just as easily have gone somewhere else.

26 VIC. No, no . . . I've enjoyed tonight.

14

1   INGRID. So have I. [*There is a pause.* INGRID *wants* VIC *to kiss her but he can't pluck up the courage.*] It must be getting late. I shall have to go. [*They get up.*] If you leave me here you can cut back through the park.

2   VIC. I'll take you all the way.

3   INGRID. It's only round the corner.

4   VIC. Okay . . . I'll see you tomorrow, then.

5   INGRID. Yes, see you tomorrow. [INGRID *hesitates again, waiting for* VIC *to kiss her goodnight, but again he muffs it.*] I'll say good-night, then.

6   VIC. Yes . . . goodnight.

    INGRID *moves away.*

7   INGRID. Goodnight.

8   VIC. Goodnight. [*He walks slowly backwards as* INGRID *goes almost off.*] I say . . .

9   INGRID. What?

10 VIC. Happy New Year!

11 INGRID [*laughs*]. Happy New Year.

    She goes right off and VIC *continues to walk backwards until finally he turns round and exits doing a happy little jig.*

    SCENE 5   THE BROWNS' LIVING-ROOM
                 Early evening

ARTHUR *is at table, having tea.* VIC *is standing, ready to go out, and drinking last cup of tea on his feet.* MRS. BROWN, *who rarely sits down with the others, is moving about between cooker and table.*

12 MRS. BROWN. If you've got everything you want I'll have a cup of tea. [*She picks up teapot and pours.*]

13 ARTHUR. Aye, do, and sit down with it. You're allus on the go.

14 MRS. BROWN. I have to be, with you two to look after.

15 ARTHUR. There's one less now, there should be less to do.

1   MRS. BROWN. Our Christine used to help, not expect to be waited on hand and foot. [*She is about to sit down.*]

2   ARTHUR. We could do with some more bread.

3   MRS. BROWN. There you are, y'see.

She goes over and starts cutting bread as VIC *straightens his tie* [ARTHUR's *tie actually*] *in the mirror.*

4   ARTHUR. I'd like to wear that tie meself sometimes.

5   VIC. Okay, let me know and I'll lend it to you.

6   ARTHUR. What's up with your own ties?

7   VIC. The stripes go the wrong way. [*There is a knock at the door.*] Okay, I'll go.

VIC *goes into passage and opens door.*

8   MR. VAN HUYTEN. Good evening, Victor.

9   VIC. Hello, Mr. Van Huyten. Come in, come in.

VIC *comes in with* MR. VAN HUYTEN, *an old man who is almost quaint in his correctness of manners, speech and appearance. His habitual dress is black jacket and striped trousers.*

10   VIC. Look who's called to see us.

MR. VAN HUYTEN *nods at the* BROWNS.

11   MR. VAN HUYTEN. Mrs. Brown, Mr. Brown . . . I hope you're keeping well.

12   ARTHUR. Can't grumble, Mr. Van Huyten. How's yourself?

13   MR. VAN HUYTEN. I keep active, you know . . . But I'm afraid I've interrupted your meal.

14   ARTHUR. Don't you worry about that. You know you're welcome here any time. Sit yerself down.

VIC *gives* MR. VAN HUYTEN *a seat.*

15   MRS. BROWN. Can I offer you a cup of tea, Mr. Van Huyten? There's a pot fresh made.

16   MR. VAN HUYTEN. No, no, no, Mrs. Brown. Thank you very

much. I won't stay but I called to see Victor. I would have contacted you earlier, but a big batch of records arrived this afternoon and it was nearly closing time before I remembered. I've unexpectedly got a couple of tickets for a concert at the Town Hall and I wondered if you'd like to go.

2 VIC. When's that, then, Mr. Van Huyten?

3 MR. VAN HUYTEN. It's tonight actually.

4 VIC. Tonight. Oh, what a pity. I've got something else on. [VIC *is genuinely disappointed but he has a date with* INGRID.] Is it a good programme?

5 MR. VAN HUYTEN. I don't know all the details but I believe they're doing the Beethoven Seventh.

6 ARTHUR. We once won t'second section at Belle Vue with Beethoven's works. ['*Beethoven's Works' is one piece to* ARTHUR *and he pronounces the name as written.*] That'd be thirty-five or thirty-six. We had a good band at that time.

7 MRS. BROWN. You're not doing owt so important you can't put it off, are you, Victor?

8 VIC. I can't promise to meet people and just not turn up.

9 MR. VAN HUYTEN. No indeed. Don't break an appointment, Victor. It's very short notice, I know. I often get complimentary tickets, you know. I'm sure there'll be another time.

10 VIC. I hope so.

11 ARTHUR. Beethoven's Works. Then there was Rossini Delights and Gems from Webber . . . We used to play 'em all.

12 MR. VAN HUYTEN. Perhaps I could invite you to join me, Mr. Brown. That is, if Mrs. Brown has no objections.

13 MRS. BROWN. He's welcome to go for me, Mr. Van Huyten.

14 VIC. Aye, why don't you go, Dad? Listen to some right music for a change.

1 ARTHUR. Right music? What you talking about? I've *played* more music than you've ever listened to. Have you ever sat in the middle of t'massed bands and played 'Finlandia'—wi' a choir an' all? No, you haven't, so don't talk to me about music.

2 VIC. Aye, I know, Dad. I'm only pulling your leg. It's smashing ... Anyway, how are things at the shop, Mr. Van Huyten?

3 MR. VAN HUYTEN. Business is very good.

4 MRS. BROWN. Is our Victor any help to you on Saturday mornings?

5 MR. VAN HUYTEN. Oh, yes, indeed. But I'm afraid the afternoons are becoming more than I can cope with. It's all these young people wanting their pop records. I'd like to find somebody to help me out then as well.

6 VIC. All day Saturday, do you mean? I could do that, if you like.

7 MR. VAN HUYTEN. I'd certainly be pleased to have you, Victor. If you could come in all day on Saturdays that would be splendid.

8 VIC. Tell you what, I'll pop round and see you during the week and we'll talk about it. I shall have to be off now.

9 ARTHUR. All these symphony orchestra brass players, they're all trained in brass bands, y'know. They don't know they're born when they get into an orchestra. Sitting about doing nowt half their time. In a brass band you've got to work for your living.

10 VIC [*laughing*]. You see what you can do with him, Mr. Van Huyten. I'm off. Ta ra, everybody. [*He goes out.*]

11 MRS. BROWN. He's in a tearing hurry.

12 MR. VAN HUYTEN. Victor's a considerate young man. He wouldn't like to keep somebody waiting.

13 ARTHUR [*dryly*]. Aye, especially if it's somebody wearing a skirt.

MRS. BROWN *looks at him, surprised to realize that he knows more than she does, for once.*

SCENE 6   A STREET CORNER
Later the same evening

VIC *hurries on to find* INGRID *already waiting.*

1   VIC. I'm sorry, Ingrid, I always seem to be late. Somebody dropped in and I couldn't get away.

2   INGRID. It's all right. I haven't been here long. Vic, I've brought my friend along. I hope you don't mind.

VIC *hasn't noticed the girl on the other side of* INGRID *but now he looks at her, considerably taken aback.*

3   VIC. Oh . . . er, no, that's okay.

4   INGRID. Vic, this is Dorothy; Dorothy, Vic.

5   DOROTHY [*rather challengingly*]. Hello.

6   VIC. How d'ye do?

7   DOROTHY. Do you know a girl called Mary Fitzpatrick?

8   VIC. Eh? Yes, I know her.

9   DOROTHY. You don't know me, though, do you?

10   VIC. I don't think so.

11   DOROTHY. I know you, though; and I know Mary Fitz-patrick.

12   VIC [*bored by her*]. Do you? Well give her my love next time you see her.

13   DOROTHY. You used to give it to her yourself at one time, didn't you?

14   VIC. Mary Fitzpatrick? I hardly knew her.

15   INGRID [*breaking in*]. Where shall we go, then?

16   DOROTHY. They say the Plaza's ever so good this week.

17   INGRID. Would you like to go there, Vic?

VIC *doesn't want to go anywhere with* DOROTHY.

18   VIC. I'm easy.

19   INGRID. Well, shall we walk round that way and then decide?

1 VIC. Okay. [DOROTHY *begins to stroll off one way and* VIC *hesitates.*] Isn't it quicker this way?

2 DOROTHY. I was going to show you where Ralph Wilson lives now, Ingrid.

3 INGRID. Is it round here?

4 DOROTHY. Yes, just down the road. Ever so posh, it is. He's too stuck up for words these days.

5 INGRID. They were always well off. And he's friendly enough with me when I see him.

6 DOROTHY. Well he should be friendly with you, if anybody.

7 INGRID. What d'you mean?

8 DOROTHY. I mean after that time you were locked in the tennis-club changing room with him.

9 INGRID. You know very well it was Harry Norris who did that. He had the key all the time.

10 DOROTHY. But you didn't seem bothered about getting out so quick, either of you.

11 INGRID. That was what everybody wanted, wasn't it, for us to make a fuss.

12 DOROTHY. All except Ralph Wilson. I think he put Harry Norris up to it in the first place.

13 INGRID. Well he didn't get anything out of it if he did.

14 DOROTHY. That's not what he told the other lads afterwards.

15 INGRID. I don't know why you should bring this old gossip up. Vic isn't interested.

16 DOROTHY. Perhaps he ought to be.

17 VIC [*suddenly flaring*]. You're everybody's friend, aren't you?

18 DOROTHY. What d'you mean by that?

19 VIC. First you try it on me, and now it's Ingrid.

20 DOROTHY. Who do you think *you* are? I know things about *you* that you wouldn't want spreading about.

1 VIC. You don't know anything about me, and if you're thinking of inventing something you'd better think again.

2 DOROTHY. Why, what will you do?

3 VIC. I'll tell you what I'll do. I'll take your pants down and slap your arse.

4 DOROTHY. You lay a finger on me and I'll call the police.

5 VIC. The bloke that laid a finger on you'ud deserve a medal. You'd need a bag over your head before anybody'd take *you* into a tennis pavilion.

6 DOROTHY. You, you rotten devil . . .

DOROTHY *dissolves into tears and begins to walk away.*

7 INGRID. You shouldn't have said that.

8 VIC. Oh, what the hell. She asked for it.

9 INGRID. She's crying.

10 VIC. Are you going with her or with me?

11 INGRID. I can't leave her now.

12 VIC. After what she said about you? Why did you bring her with you, anyway?

13 INGRID. She came round for tea and I didn't want to send her away on her own. She's my best friend.

14 VIC. You could have fooled me.

15 INGRID. She's very sensitive really. I shall have to go to her.

16 VIC. All right, go on, then.

17 INGRID. Will I see you at work on Monday?

18 VIC. I'm usually there.

19 INGRID. Goodnight, then.

20 VIC [*coldly*]. Goodnight.

INGRID *goes off after* DOROTHY. VIC *kicks angrily at the pavement as the scene fades.*

SCENE 7   THE DRAWING OFFICE
            Morning, before starting time

VIC *is already there working as* WILLY *comes in, yawning.*

1 VIC. Now then, Willy.

2 WILLY. Hello, Vic. What you doing here so early? Wet the bed or something?

3 VIC. Aw, just thought I'd get an early start. Hassop's been on about that extension again.

4 WILLY. What a bloody awful time of day. It's funny, the blokes on the shop floor have been at it for an hour already.

5 VIC. Aye, we don't know we're born, do we? What you doing here at this time, anyway?

6 WILLY. Clocks. We've got three in the house and every one of 'em's got blood pressure. You have to wedge a bit of cardboard under the one on the mantelpiece, the one in the kitchen gains an hour in every three and the alarm only works if you lie it face down, and then the bell doesn't ring. I was on the bus an hour early this morning so I walked about a bit, then had a cup of tea, and here I am. [*yawns*] Got a fag?

7 VIC. Didn't have time to buy any, eh? Here, catch.

He throws a cigarette to WILLY, *who lights up.*

8 WILLY. You don't look so perky, mate. Didn't she turn up?

9 VIC. Who?

10 WILLY. I don't know. Miss whoever it is.

11 VIC. She turned up all right. And she brought her friend.

12 WILLY. You should have called round for me. I'd have taken care of her friend.

13 VIC. Not this one, you wouldn't. Feet like fiddle cases and a mouth like a crack in a pie.

14 WILLY. Didn't she say why she'd brought her?

22

1 VIC. Oh, she spun me a cock and bull tale about her turning up for tea and she couldn't get rid of her without offending her. 'Course, I didn't fall for that one.

2 WILLY. Maybe you were a bit hasty for her.

3 VIC. I never laid a finger on her.

4 WILLY. Well, perhaps you were too slow, then.

5 VIC. It isn't like that.

6 WILLY. Serious, is it?

7 VIC. It looks as if it's all over.

8 WILLY. It's that young Ingrid from the typing pool, isn't it?

9 VIC. How did you know?

10 WILLY. Because I'm not blind, mate.

11 VIC. Look, Willy. I know we all kid about birds, but keep it quiet from the others, will you?

12 WILLY [seriously]. Mum's the word.

    RAWLY comes in.

13 RAWLY. 'Morning.

14 VIC. Hi.

15 WILLY. Blimey, I never thought I'd get here before you.

16 RAWLY [ignoring this]. Anybody go to the concert at the Town Hall last night?

17 WILLY. Not me, mate. I'm not cultured. I just go back to the jungle in the evening and swing about in the trees.

18 RAWLY. I saw old Mr. Van Huyten and wondered if Vic had been.

19 VIC. No, I'd've liked to but I couldn't make it.

20 RAWLY. Fantastic. It's tragic to think he never actually heard the greater part of his own music.

21 WILLY. Who's that?

22 RAWLY. Beethoven.

23 WILLY. How's that? Did he snuff it young, or summat?

24 RAWLY. He was stone deaf.

    CONROY enters, holding a few letters in his hand.

1 CONROY. 'Morning, slaves.

2 VIC. Hello.

3 WILLY. 'Morning.

4 RAWLY. He went deaf before he'd written most of his major
   works.

5 CONROY. Who's this, then—John Lennon?

6 RAWLY. Beethoven.

7 WILLY. Well how could he compose music if he was deaf?

8 RAWLY. It was all in his mind. He just had to write it down.

9 VIC. Without hearing it?

10 RAWLY. Of course. A composer has no need to actually hear
   the music to put it down on paper. And a musician
   of the first rank can read an orchestral score as easily
   as the average person reads a book.

11 VIC. And it's his own fault if he hears a wrong note, eh?

12 RAWLY. Exactly. In fact some musicians so despair of hearing
   the perfect performance of their favourite work that
   they give up listening to music and read scores instead.

13 CONROY. Like playing with yourself because you can't find
   the perfect woman. [*They all laugh, and* RAWLY *looks at his
   watch uncomfortably and starts work.* CONROY *looks through the
   letters.*] Now what have we here? Special delivery for
   Mr. V. Brown. Sorry! V. Brown, *Esquire*! [VIC *goes to take it,
   but* CONROY *pulls it back.*] Eager beaver! Let's guess who it's
   from. [*He sniffs at the envelope.*] What exotic cloud is this
   that makes my senses reel?

   VIC *snatches the envelope away.*

14 VIC. Give it here.

15 CONROY. All right, mate, we all know you've got a girl
   friend.

16 VIC. Who says? What the hell's it got to do with you?

17 CONROY. We know you're doing a bit for our Miss Rothwell,
   the siren of the typing pool.

18 VIC. Why don't you mind your own business, Conroy?

19 CONROY. You want to be careful there, young Browny. She's

24

a hot bit o' stuff, our Miss Rothwell. Know what her nickname is? They call her the Praying Mantis. You know what one of them is, don't you? It's an insect like a big grasshopper, and the female eats the male while they're actually on the job together. Just gobbles him up, bit by bit.

2 VIC. Ah, you've got a mind like a sewer, Conroy.

3 CONROY. And guess which bit she leaves till last!

The starting bell sounds.

4 WILLY. Time to sharpen your pencils. [VIC *starts to read the letter and a smile comes to his face.*] You know, it's a funny thing, but no bird ever writes me a letter.

5 VIC [*grins*]. Mebbe they know you can't read.

WILLY *pulls a face at* VIC *who goes on smiling happily as he puts the letter back in the envelope.*

SCENE 8   THE PARK
           That night

VIC *is sitting on a bench. He get up as* INGRID *hurries on.*

6 INGRID. Hello. Am I late?

7 VIC. No, I'm early this time.

8 INGRID. You got my letter?

9 VIC. Yes, I got it.

They sit down.

10 INGRID. I wasn't sure you'd be able to get away.

11 VIC. It was a bit tricky. We've all been over to my sister's new flat. They just got back from their honeymoon yesterday and we all had to go to tea.

12 INGRID. You know, I didn't want her to come, Vic. Only she sometimes just pops in and stays. I couldn't get rid of her. She said she'd just come and say hello and then go.

1　VIC. I thought you'd brought her as a hint to me.

2　INGRID [*laughing*]. Oh, Vic!

3　VIC. I suppose it was being upset that made me let fly at her like that. I thought you didn't want to see me again and you didn't like telling me to my face.

4　INGRID. And it wasn't that way at all. Doesn't it just show how misunderstandings can come about? It's a good job I did write that letter or you might not have asked me out again.

5　VIC. Would you have been bothered?

6　INGRID. What do you think?

7　VIC. I think you ought to come a bit closer. [*They move closer together on the seat and* VIC *puts his arm round her.*] Hmmm, I like your perfume.

8　INGRID. It's called 'Desire'.

9　VIC. Living dangerously, aren't you, wearing stuff like that?

10　INGRID. I only wear it on special occasions.

11　VIC. That's just as well I should think.

12　INGRID. I mean, it's not for everyday use. It's too expensive.

13　VIC. I don't know whether to be flattered or not.

14　INGRID. Why?

15　VIC. I don't know whether it means you trust me to behave or trust me not to.

16　INGRID [*laughs*]. Hey, what's that in your pocket?

17　VIC. Oh . . . It's a book. [*He takes it out.*] David lent it me. Chris's husband.

18　INGRID [*glancing at title*]. 'For whom the bell tolls.'*

19　VIC. Have you read it?

20　INGRID. I just can't read books. There isn't the time when you've got the telly. I have three magazines a week and I can't get through *them*.

21　VIC. They made a film of it once, with Gary Cooper and Ingrid Bergman.

* A very well-known book by the American Nobel Prize-Winner, Ernest Hemingway.

1 INGRID. I'm called after Ingrid Bergman. Mother was mad on her at one time.

2 VIC. I thought it was an unusual name for an English girl.

3 INGRID. Would you rather I was called Mary or Barbara, or something like that?

4 VIC. Dorothy—that's a name I've always liked.

5 INGRID. Go on with you.

6 VIC. No, as a matter of fact, I like you just the way you are.

7 INGRID [*looking straight at him*]. Do you, Vic?

8 VIC. Shall I show you?

He puts his arms round her and kisses her. When they break INGRID *gives a little laugh.*

9 INGRID. Hold on a minute. Let me take a breath.

10 VIC. To think that Dorothy nearly spoiled everything.

11 INGRID. Actually, she's jealous, that's her trouble.

12 VIC. Why doesn't she get a chap of her own?

13 INGRID. She pretends she doesn't like men.

14 VIC. Don't they ever ask her out?

15 INGRID. I don't think so. Anyway, she's not really attractive, is she? You didn't find her attractive, did you?

16 VIC. I find you attractive. [*They go into a really heavy embrace.*] Gosh, I'm crazy about you, Ingrid.

17 INGRID. Oh, Vic, Vic. [VIC *puts his hand inside her coat and in a moment* INGRID *covers it with her own hand, holding it there rather than attempting to remove it.* Oh, Vic, we can't. We mustn't.

18 VIC [*tenderly*]. I know. I know.

They kiss again with passion.

19 INGRID. Vic, you don't think I'm common, do you?

20 VIC. No, you mustn't think that. It's not like that at all. I love you, Ingrid. I love you.

SCENE 9   THE BROWNS' LIVING-ROOM
Later the same night

CHRISTINE *is in the room with* MRS. BROWN *when* VIC *comes in, whistling.*

1   MRS. BROWN. You're here, then. And sounding very pleased
with yourself.

2   VIC. Hello. Chris. What are you doing here?

3   CHRISTINE. I just popped round to borrow the scales.

4   MRS. BROWN. I'll get 'em for you now. [*She goes off into scullery.*]

5   VIC. What's up with her?

6   CHRISTINE. She's feeling a bit mouldy because you dashed
off as soon as you'd swallowed your tea.

7   VIC. I made it all right with you, didn't I?

8   CHRISTINE. Oh yes, but you know how she goes on sometimes. She thought you might have offended me and
David.

9   VIC. I sometimes think she's fast for something to grumble
about.

CHRISTINE *regards him with amusement.*

10   CHRISTINE. Anyway, was it worth it?

11   VIC. What? Oh, yes, yes.

12   CHRISTINE. What's her name?

13   VIC. Oh, it's just a girl from the office. Why I can't take a
bird out without feeling like a criminal, I don't know.

14   CHRISTINE. Perhaps if you told Mother about her . . .

15   VIC. You know how she goes on, Chris. She'd have us
posting the banns before we knew where we were.

16   CHRISTINE [*amused*]. I know, I've had some.

17   VIC. The real trouble is she somehow makes you ashamed
of normal feelings. You know, sort of dirty. It's something nobody talks about except to make mucky jokes
in the office and *she* seems to see it as something you've

got to put up with because it makes the world go on. I wonder sometimes how she ever got us.

2 CHRISTINE [*laughs*]. She collected Co-op checks, didn't you know?

3 VIC. And I suppose she's giving all hers to you now, eh?

4 CHRISTINE. Yes, she's dropping hints about that. [*laughs*]

5 VIC. You see, I wouldn't mind getting married and settling down in a place of me own, but it'd have to be something as good as you and David have got.

6 CHRISTINE. I've been lucky, Vic. I'm in danger of getting smug.

7 VIC. No, not you, love.

MRS. BROWN *returns with the kitchen scales.*

8 MRS. BROWN. Here we are. I had to dust 'em. It's ages since I used 'em. Do you want me to wrap a bit of paper round them?

9 CHRISTINE. No, they'll be all right like that. Perhaps one day I'll have everything I need without having to borrow.

10 MRS. BROWN. You'll be lucky if you do. There's allus summat you're short of no matter how long you've been married. And some things you've too many of.

11 CHRISTINE [*smiling*]. Like water sets.

12 MRS. BROWN. Aye. I thought your Auntie Ivy could have done better for you than a jug and half a dozen glasses from Woolworth's.

13 CHRISTINE. They were very nice, though.

14 MRS. BROWN. She could have done better if she'd put her hand down a bit further.

15 CHRISTINE. Anyway, I'll be off or David'll wonder where I've got to.

16 VIC. Do you want me to walk round with you?

17 CHRISTINE. No, I'll be all right. It's only a few minutes. I'll see you later, then.

18 MRS. BROWN. Yes, goodnight, love.

19 VIC. 'Night, Chris.

CHRISTINE *goes out and* MRS. BROWN *looks disapprovingly at* VIC.

1 MRS. BROWN. And what have you got to say for yourself?

2 VIC. Eh?

3 MRS. BROWN. Getting invited out for your tea and then sloping off like that. I don't know what David thought to you, I'm sure.

4 VIC. I told our Chris, y'know.

5 MRS. BROWN. Oh, she'll stick up for you. She allus did.

6 VIC. Look, I went to tea at me own sister's, not Buckingham Palace. I didn't have to stay till bedtime and I explained it to Chris.

7 MRS. BROWN. Explained what? I don't know where you've been that was so important.

8 VIC. I had a date.

9 MRS. BROWN. But you knew a week ago that you'd be at our Christine's today.

10 VIC. There was a bit of a mix up.

11 MRS. BROWN. It's all mixed up to me. Hole-in-the-corner work. Do I know this lass you've been out with?

12 VIC. No.

A pause.

13 MRS. BROWN. Well what's wrong? Are you ashamed of her or summat?

14 VIC. No, I'm not, but I don't want you to go getting ideas.

15 MRS. BROWN. What sort of ideas?

16 VIC. That it's serious, or anything.

17 MRS. BROWN. I don't know how it is with young folk nowadays. They just want to play fast and loose with one another. In my young days we either courted properly or left it alone.

18 VIC. You know what they say—play the field before you're married and you won't want to after.

19 MRS. BROWN. There's a lot of folk got married quicker than they thought they would through playing t'field.

Two scenes from the film version of A Kind of Loving *starring Alan Bates as Vic, June Ritchie as Ingrid and Thora Hird as Mrs. Rothwell. Above: Act One, Scene 7   Below: Act Two, Scene 4*

Six scenes from the 1968 stage production at the York Theatre Royal

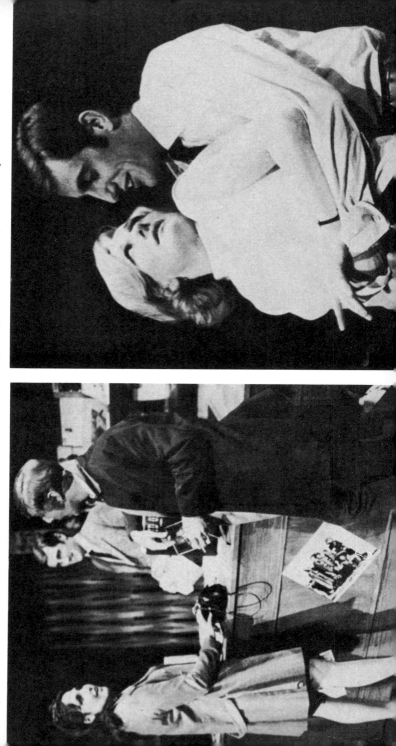

Page 40, speech 6   WILLY I'm telling you. What about it.

Page 46, speech 11   INGRID No, I don't want to pack it in.

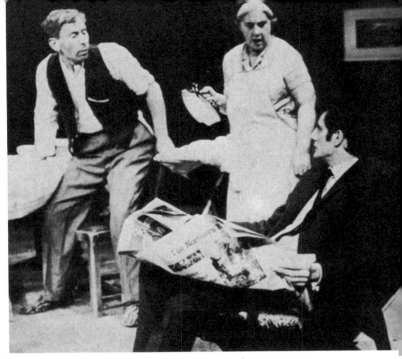

Page 53, speech 6   MRS BROWN *You fool. You gret silly fool.*

Page 59, speech 12   MR ROTHWELL *I think we shall all get on together, don't you?*

69, speech 15   VIC *All right, then, stop in and wear your bloody coat.*

84, speech 15   INGRID *We'll find a kind of loving to carry us through.*

MRS. BROWN *exits on this line, leaving* VIC *to throw up his hands in exasperation.*

SCENE 10   THE DRAWING OFFICE
Near the end of lunchtime

A large sheet of drawing paper has been pinned to the end of RAWLY's *board with a message on it in Indian ink:*

'RAWLY'S KULTURE KORNER, ARTISTIC ADVICE FREELY GIVEN, 9 TO 5.30 SHARP.'

VIC *and* WILLY *are laughing at this as* RAWLY *comes in.*

1 RAWLY. Yes, very funny indeed. Am I supposed to guess who's responsible? [*He begins to remove the notice.*]

2 VIC. There's no prizes.

3 RAWLY. You all think he's a scream, don't you? [*to* VIC] Well, he's no friend of yours.

4 VIC. Oh, how's that?

5 RAWLY. He was talking about you in the canteen, you and that Rothwell girl.

6 VIC. Oh yes?

7 RAWLY. Yes, he said something about grasshoppers. He said she calls you by rubbing her legs together.

8 VIC. Why you—

9 WILLY. Ah, don't bother with that little stirrer, Vic. He's only trying to make trouble between you and Conroy.

CONROY *walks in.*

10 CONROY. Did I hear somebody talking about me?

11 VIC. Aye, I was just saying I'd bought a pig and I didn't know what to call it.

CONROY *is incensed at this. He makes for* VIC.

12 CONROY. You cheeky young bleeder. I'll knock your bloody head off your shoulders.

31

1 WILLY. Hey, steady on!

2 VIC. You've got it coming, Conroy.

   They grapple with each other.

3 WILLY. Get him down, Vic, then you'll have a chance. [VIC *and* CONROY *go down.*] That's more like it. Now thump his earhole.

   The door opens suddenly and HASSOP *walks in.*

4 HASSOP. And what's all this about, might I ask? Come on, get up, both of you. [VIC *and* CONROY *disengage and get up, brushing down their clothes.*] I don't want any more of this—understand? I won't have the office turned into a monkey house. You come here to work and get the job done and if you don't like the arrangement you can take your hook somewhere else. You're old enough to know better, Conroy, and it's time you grew up. As for you, Brown, I'm not sure. You'd better get your ideas straightened out and look to your work if you want to stay with us. I don't know what you were scrapping about and I don't want to know. But don't let me see any more of it.

   CONROY *is bored by the lengths to which* HASSOP *is going.*

5 CONROY. I don't see what all the fuss is about.

6 HASSOP. What's that?

7 CONROY. I don't see why there should be such a fuss over a bit of alecking about.

8 HASSOP. If you don't like the way this office is run, Conroy, you know what you can do. Now get to your boards, both of you, and get on with some work. [HASSOP *walks away.*]

9 VIC. I'm sorry about that, Conroy. I started it.

10 CONROY. Oh, forget about it. I've needled you often enough. I didn't know you were serious about that bird.

11 VIC. It depends what you call serious.

12 CONROY [*shrewdly*]. And what you want out of a bird.

13 VIC. Yeh, that's just the point.

1 CONROY. She's a good-looking lass.

2 VIC. Oh, she's a nice enough kid as well, if it comes to that.

3 CONROY. Well, that's your problem, mate. Mine's getting out of this hole. If Hassop thinks I'm stopping here to be talked to like a lad, he's got another think coming. [*He strides round to* RAWLY's *place.*] Where's that *Daily Telegraph* of yours, Rawly?

4 RAWLY. You can have it at half-past five.

5 CONROY. To hell with that. I want it now.

   RAWLY *reluctantly passes the newspaper.*

6 RAWLY. I won't be responsible if—

7 CONROY. Do us a favour, mate, and drop dead. [*He takes the paper to his own place and opens it wide on his board, calmly turning the pages.*] Situations vacant . . . Draughtsmen and Designers . . .

   VIC *is looking at* CONROY *in something like admiration now.*

8 VIC. He can see you from his office, y'know. You'll have him on your neck again in a minute.

9 CONROY. I don't give a damn. The trouble with you, young Browny, is you knuckle under too easy.

   HASSOP *appears at* CONROY's *elbow.*

10 HASSOP. I said get on with some work, Conroy. This is a drawing office, not a reading room. [CONROY *ignores him.*] I'm talking to you, Conroy.

11 CONROY. And I'm looking for a job. And if I don't find one in here I'll look in the *Yorkshire Post* and the *Guardian*. I've had enough of this bloody lot and I'm getting out. I'm not one of your frightened little time-servers, cowering over his board every time he hears the boss's voice. I'm a lad 'at knows a thing or two and I'm taking me talents elsewhere. There's firms crying out for blokes who can think for themselves, and they're paying more than this sweatshop an' all.

12 HASSOP. You'll be applying for a new job sooner than you think if you carry on like this.

1 CONROY. You sack me if you want to. You'll be doing me a favour.

HASSOP trembles with rage but CONROY'S *audacity is momentarily too much for him. He wags his finger at* CONROY.

2 HASSOP. I'll see you later. [*He strides away to his office.*]

CONROY *looks at* VIC.

3 CONROY. Remember the motto, young Browny. Nil illegitimum carborundum.

4 VIC. Eh?

5 CONROY. Don't let the bastards grind you down.

SCENE 11   THE PARK
Night

VIC *and* INGRID *are sitting on the bench.*

6 INGRID. You're sighing.

7 VIC. Am I?

8 INGRID. There's nothing wrong, is there?

9 VIC. Wrong?

10 INGRID. I mean . . . you're not sorry . . . about just now?

He is, but he can't discuss it.

11 VIC. This rotten, lousy weather . . .

12 INGRID. You're not in a very good mood tonight, are you?

13 VIC. I hadn't noticed.

14 INGRID. I have. Is it something I've said or done?

15 VIC. 'Course it isn't.

16 INGRID. There is something wrong, though, isn't there?

17 VIC. I'm a bit fed up all round. I'm not very happy at work these days.

18 INGRID. Perhaps you ought to look for another job.

19 VIC. Yeh. I think Mr. Van Huyten would like me to go into the shop full time.

1   INGRID. Whew, selling records for a living? Do you want to?

2   VIC. It's interesting. I like it. There's more to it than that, you know.

3   INGRID. It's not as good a job as being a draughtsman, though, is it?

4   VIC. I suppose not. Still it's worth a drop in wages if you're doing what you want to do. And Mr. Van Huyten would see me all right. He's a nice feller.

5   INGRID. Well you're a man now so you can make your own decisions. [VIC *gives a sardonic little laugh at this*.] Did you get my card yesterday?

6   VIC. Oh yes, thanks very much.

7   INGRID [*opening her handbag*]. I've got something else for you here. [*She hands him a small package.*]

8   VIC. What is it?

9   INGRID. Open it and see.

VIC *opens the package and finds a wrist watch.*

10 VIC. Whatever it is . . . Oh, that's marvellous!

11 INGRID. It was time you had a new one.

VIC *is embarrassed both by the generosity itself and by its happening at this stage in their relationship.*

12 VIC. But it must have cost a fortune. I don't deserve anything like this.

13 INGRID. I always believe in giving nice presents. There's no point unless it's something worthwhile.

14 VIC. It's smashing . . .

15 INGRID. You won't have any excuse for being late now.

16 VIC. No . . .

17 INGRID. What else did you get?

18 VIC. Me mother and dad bought me this cigarette case. Isn't it a beauty?

19 INGRID. Yes, it's lovely.

20 VIC. Me dad bought me a new tie as well. Said it might stop me wearing his. And Chris and David gave me some

cuff-links and a record. An L.P. of Tchaikovsky's
Pathetic Symphony.

2   INGRID. A symphony? I didn't know you were such a
     highbrow.

3   VIC. I'm not. I suppose it's come from going into the shop.
     You get to want to hear some music that's worth
     repeating. It grows on you.

4   INGRID. It's all highbrow stuff to me.

5   VIC. It was written for people to enjoy, wasn't it? What's
     wrong with me enjoying it?

6   INGRID. There's lots of people pretend to like that sort of
     thing because they think it makes them Somebody.

7   VIC. Aye, like Rawly. But you know me better than that.

8   INGRID. Personally, I can't stand all that dreary stuff. I like
     something with a tune.

     VIC *is becoming impatient with her ignorance and stupidity.*

9   VIC. But there's bags of tunes in Tchaikovsky. Great big
     tunes. You want to give it a try sometime.

10 INGRID. I don't think I'll bother. I know what I like, and I'm
     sorry if I don't come up to expectations.

     Her taking it all personally, added to her ignorance, only confirms
     VIC's *growing fears about her.*

11 VIC. It's not that, only you can't expect everybody to be
     like you, can you?

12 INGRID. I'm sure I don't want to fall out about it.

13 VIC. Who's falling out? I'm only saying ... Oh, never mind.
     We'd better let it drop.

14 INGRID. I think we better had. [*awkward silence*] Now you're
     sighing again.

15 VIC. Sorry.

16 INGRID. You are all right, aren't you?

17 VIC. Yes. I'm okay.

18 INGRID. I thought at first ... you know, earlier on ... that
     you wanted to ... well, go all the way.

1   VIC. I suppose I did.

2   INGRID. Have you ever done it, you know, with anybody else?

3   VIC. No.

4   INGRID. I wondered.

5   VIC. I wouldn't have gone as far as that if you hadn't let me know.

6   INGRID. Let you know? How did I let you know?

7   VIC. Kissing me that way.

8   INGRID. I thought you loved me. Don't you?

9   VIC. I don't know.

10   INGRID. Do you love anybody else?

11   VIC. No.

12   INGRID. You don't think *I've* ever gone as far as that with anybody else, do you? Is that the kind of girl you think I am?

13   VIC. How should I know? [*a pause*] No, I didn't mean that. I know you're not that kind of girl.

14   INGRID. I am now though, aren't I?

15   VIC. Come off it.

16   INGRID. Have you just been thinking I'm easy?

17   VIC. No. No, it's not like that. I can't explain, that's all. I just can't explain.

18   INGRID [*at a loss*]. Anyway, I don't think it's wrong. Not when you're fond of the person.

19   VIC. No . . . not when you're fond of the person.

    The lights fade

SCENE 12   MR. VAN HUYTEN'S RECORD SHOP

A counter, some racks of brightly coloured record sleeves, and a cubicle where customers may play records. There is a GIRL in the cubicle as the curtain goes up and we can faintly hear the record she is listening to. It stops almost immediately and she comes out and approaches VIC behind the counter.

1 VIC. Did you like that?

2 GIRL. It's not really what I want. Have you got anything else by him?

3 VIC. There's quite a few in this rack here. Here, try this one if you don't know it. [*Hands her a record.*]

4 GIRL [*looking at sleeve*]. Ta, I will.

She wanders back into cubicle as MR. VAN HUYTEN *comes through from back premises.*

5 MR. VAN HUYTEN. Everything all right, Victor?

6 VIC. Fine, Mr. Van Huyten.

7 MR. VAN HUYTEN. Good. I'll leave you with it for a while, if you don't mind. I must get to the bank.

8 VIC. Righto. Take your time.

As MR. VAN HUYTEN *goes out*, WILLY *comes in.*

9 WILLY. Now then, have you got anything by that deaf genius Rawly Von Beethoven?

10 VIC [*pleased to see him*]. Willy. I was wondering when you'd look me up.

11 WILLY. Thought I'd better see how you were making out. How's it going?

12 VIC. Fine, Willy, fine.

13 WILLY. No regrets, then?

14 VIC. No, why should I have?

15 WILLY. Well, some people might say it's not as good a trade as draughtsmanship, that's all.

16 VIC. This isn't like working in any old shop, Willy. Mr. Van Huyten's an old friend of the family.

17 WILLY. Aye, you said so. Well it makes a change I suppose. I feel like one myself. The old place isn't the same at all with both you and Conroy gone.

18 VIC. Conroy wasn't a bad bloke, you know, when you got to know him.

19 WILLY. No, I suppose not. They reckon old Hassop tried to get him to change his mind and stay on. And I always thought he hated his guts.

1 VIC. He knew he was losing a good man. He didn't mind so much when I left. I'm not in Conroy's class as a draughtsman.

2 WILLY. I've just seen your girl friend up the street.

3 VIC. Who?

4 WILLY. Young Ingrid. You're still knocking about with her, aren't you?

5 VIC. I take her out now and again. Haven't seen her lately.

6 WILLY. Don't sound so enthusiastic about it or you'll bust a gut.

7 VIC. You know, Willy, it's a funny thing with her. Sometimes I can't keep away from her and other times I can hardly bear the sight of her. Sometimes I can't keep my mind on anything for thinking about her. Other times I wish I'd never see her again.

8 WILLY. Well, you don't have to get tied up. Take what's going and leave it at that, that's always been my motto.

9 VIC. No, look, I'm talking serious now, Willy. I know we all used to reckon in the office that birds were useful for one thing, but there's a time when you want something more than that. I thought I had it with Ingrid at first. Then all of a sudden I realized I didn't even like her very much.

10 WILLY. You don't have to like a bird to get her into bed.

11 VIC. Aagh, I just get bloody disgusted with meself sometimes.

12 WILLY. You know, your trouble is you're too flaming—

The GIRL *interrupts him by coming out of the cubicle.* WILLY *immediately preens himself to chat her up.*

13 GIRL. I'll take this one.

VIC *takes the record and money, puts the record in a bag and notes the sale.*

14 WILLY. Haven't I seen you at the Gala Rooms, darling?

15 GIRL. You might have. I've been there.

16 WILLY. Will you be there tonight?

1   GIRL. Might be. Depends how I feel.

2   WILLY. I'm going to see The Demons in Bradford.

3   GIRL. You're lucky, aren't you? I thought they'd been booked up for weeks.

4   WILLY. I could find room for another one if you want to go.

5   GIRL. Who're you kidding?

6   WILLY. I'm telling you. What about it?

7   GIRL. How're you getting there?

8   WILLY. Borrowing the old man's car.

9   GIRL. You'd better pull the other one. It's got bells on.

10 WILLY. Tell you what. I'll meet you at the corner of Market Street at seven.

11 GIRL. I'll think about it.

12 WILLY. Seven sharp, though. Time and Willy wait for no one.

13 GIRL. I'll ask me mam.

14 WILLY. As long as you don't bring her with you, love.

The GIRL *goes out.*

15 VIC. Your old feller hasn't got a car, has he?

16 WILLY. No, and I haven't got any tickets for The Demons, either.

17 VIC. You're a right old chatter-up, aren't you?

18 WILLY. Cast your bread upon the waters, that's my system. You're set up, mate. That Ingrid. It's common knowledge she's mad about you. You want to make the best of it.

19 VIC. Aw, I dunno. It's not fair, somehow, blowing hot and cold like that. I thought when I left Whittaker's I might make a clean break. Out of sight, out of mind.

20 WILLY. Catch me wasting a chance like that. You want to get on with it, man. Just remember the motto, that's all.

21 VIC. What's that?

22 WILLY. Be prepared.

23 VIC. I'd never have the nerve to go into a shop and ask.

1   WILLY. You just walk in.

2   VIC. Where?

3   WILLY. A chemist's.

4   VIC. Suppose a bird comes to serve you?

5   WILLY. So what? She knows what they're for just like
    anybody else.

6   VIC. I couldn't ask a bird, Willy. I'd be too embarrassed.

7   WILLY. You'll have to learn sometime, won't you?

8   VIC. Aye, but . . .

9   WILLY. Aw, there's nowt to it.

10 VIC [*suspiciously*]. Not for an experienced bloke like you.

11 WILLY. Eh?

12 VIC. When did you first make it, Willy?

13 WILLY. Oh, a couple o' years ago.

14 VIC. And when was the last time?

15 WILLY. Just the other week.

16 VIC. Aye, in your flipping imagination.

17 WILLY. Look, I'll have to be off. I'll give you a ring and we'll
    fix a pint.

18 VIC [*laughing*]. Aye, and if I get any, Willy, I'll save some for
    you. [WILLY *goes out.* VIC *tidies up the counter, makes a note in a
    ledger, then goes through into back room.* INGRID *comes in.* VIC
    hears doorbell and calls out.] Be with you in a minute. [*He
    comes in and is arrested for a moment in the doorway as he sees who
    it is.*]

19 INGRID. Hello, Vic.

20 VIC. Ingrid . . . Long time no see.

21 INGRID. Yes, you're nearly a stranger. How are you liking
    your new job?

22 VIC. It's okay. I've just had Willy in for a chat.

23 INGRID. Oh. Why I called in, I was wondering if you wanted
    a ticket for the firm's dance.

24 VIC. When's that, then?

25 INGRID. Next Friday.

41

1   VIC. Should be good for a few laughs. Are you going?

2   INGRID. Yes, I expect I shall be there.

3   VIC. Will you be going on your own?

4   INGRID. I don't know yet. It depends.

5   VIC. What on? Your boy friend?

6   INGRID. Which boy friend?

7   VIC. What it is to have a choice. Well, er, suppose I buy two
    tickets and you go with me?

8   INGRID. Don't be rash; they're ten and six each.

9   VIC. Oh, you've got to be a bit reckless once in a while.

10 INGRID. Vic. [*awkwardly*] What's the matter?

11 VIC. How d'you mean?

12 INGRID. With us.

13 VIC. Nothing.

14 INGRID. Do you remember that night in the park and what
    you said?

15 VIC. Yes, I remember.

16 INGRID. Did you mean it?

17 VIC. I must have done or I wouldn't have said it. I was a bit
    carried away.

18 INGRID. You meant it then. I know you did. I don't know
    what's happened since to change it. It's not something
    I've done, is it?

19 VIC. No . . . it's . . . Oh, I don't know. Things have got a bit
    mixed up. It's no good talking about it. I don't under-
    stand it myself so I can't explain it to you.

20 INGRID. You know I've always liked you, don't you? I liked
    you since before you asked me out.

21 VIC. Yes. Yes, I know.

22 INGRID. What about now? Will you really come to the
    dance?

23 VIC. Yes. I'll give you a ring at work.

24 INGRID. You're not just saying that, are you? You will really
    ring me up?

1   VIC. Yes, I will. I promise.

2   INGRID. All right. [A MAN *comes in.*] I'd better be off, then.

3   VIC. Yes, okay. I'll see you later.

4   INGRID. Yes . . . Oh, the tickets. [*She takes the tickets from her bag and puts them on the counter.*]

5   VIC. What about the money?

6   INGRID [*at door*]. You can pay for them later.

7   VIC. Righto. See you, then. [*to* CUSTOMER] Yes, sir.

8   CUSTOMER. I just wanted to ask you about a record player.

9   VIC. Yes. Do you want it just for pops or is the quality important?

10 CUSTOMER. It's just for the youngsters, really. I want something decent but not too expensive.

11 VIC [*leading way*]. If you'd like to come through to the showroom you can see what we've got.

SCENE 13   THE ROTHWELLS' LIVING-ROOM

The doorbell rings. INGRID *straightens her hair, goes into hall and returns with* VIC.

12 VIC. Now then.

13 INGRID. I'm sorry about tonight, Vic. I was looking forward to it.

14 VIC. Oh, that's all right. I'm not mad keen on dancing, anyway. Are you all right now?

15 INGRID. Oh yes. It was only a cold but I felt rotten. But with being away from work all week I thought it wouldn't look so good me turning up at the dance.

16 VIC. Well don't worry on my account. I'm just as happy here. How long's your mum out for?

17 INGRID. All evening. She hasn't been gone long. That's

why I couldn't ring you earlier. I'd to pretend to go out for some fresh air in the end, and ring you from a box. Take your overcoat off.

2   VIC *[takes off coat and gives it to her]*. You haven't told your mother about me, then?

3   INGRID. Well, no, I haven't. I mean, it's not as if we were, well, courting, is it?

4   VIC. No . . . No, it isn't.

5   INGRID. Your parents don't know about me, do they?

6   VIC. Well, they do and they don't. They don't know how often I see you, or how it is between us.

7   INGRID. That's the trouble, isn't it? I mean, we couldn't tell anybody how it is, could we?

8   VIC. As far as anybody else is concerned we're just friends who go out with each other now and again.

9   INGRID *[mocking a little]*. Just good friends?

10   VIC. You know what I mean.

11   INGRID. I'll get some coffee. *[She goes off.]*

12   VIC. Don't make any specially.

13   INGRID *[off]*. It's ready. Only instant. I didn't grind the beans myself.

14   VIC. It's warm in here.

He takes off his jacket and drapes it over a chair. He looks round the room, coming face to face with a coloured photograph of the Queen. He gives her a gentle wave of the forearm and a waxworks smile. INGRID *returns with two cups of coffee which she puts on a table.*

15   INGRID. There we are.

16   VIC. I must say this is a bit of all right. Cosier than the park.

17   INGRID. You won't have to stay too late, that's all.

18   VIC. Don't worry about that. Do you want a fag?

19   INGRID. Please. *[*VIC *pulls cigarette case out of his pocket and a girlie book slides out after it.* INGRID *grabs it.]* Ho ho. What's this?

20   VIC *[embarrassed]*. Nothing. Let's have it.

1 INGRID [*moving quickly away*]. Not till I've had a look and seen what a mucky-minded devil you really are.

2 VIC. Come on, Ingrid.

3 INGRID [*waves the book provocatively*]. Come and get it.

VIC *half starts round a chair after her then stops.*

4 VIC. I'm not chasing you for it. [*He sits down and drinks his coffee as* INGRID *leafs through the book, giggling.*] Found anything interesting?

5 INGRID. Don't be silly. I've seen women in the nude before. I don't know how they can pose in front of a photographer like this, though.

6 VIC. It's just a job to them. Exploiting their natural assets, you might say.

7 INGRID. I'll bet there's some carrying on.

8 VIC. Now who's being mucky-minded?

9 INGRID. Well if you were taking pictures like this all day wouldn't you carry on?

10 VIC. That'd be different. I'm not used to it. I don't know where you drop on jobs like that. The blokes in the Labour Exchange must grab them for themselves.

11 INGRID [*laughs, then turns serious*]. This one's lovely though.

12 VIC. Which one? [*He goes and looks over her shoulder.*]

13 INGRID. Isn't she firm?

14 VIC. No nicer than you are.

15 INGRID. Get away. You don't mean that.

16 VIC. I do, though. I think your figure's just as good as hers. 'Course, I couldn't swear to it, like . . . I mean . . .

17 INGRID. I know what you mean. You don't have to go into details.

18 VIC [*kissing her*]. I wish we could.

19 INGRID. Could what?

20 VIC. Go into details.

21 INGRID. You want a lot, don't you?

22 VIC. You know how I am about you, Ingrid.

1   INGRID. That's the trouble. I don't know.

2   VIC. I've never felt like this about anybody before.

3   INGRID. But you don't always feel like this, do you? Then you're not bothered about me.

4   VIC. I don't know how I do feel half the time. Sometimes I feel rotten about it all and then I think it's not fair to either of us to carry on . . . I did try to break it off, y'know, when I found out it wasn't the same as I'd thought . . .

5   INGRID [*bitterly*]. But then I came running after you.

6   VIC. I wish it could be different, Ingrid.

7   INGRID. But it can't, can it?

8   VIC. I don't want to be rotten to you.

9   INGRID. I don't think you do.

10   VIC. If you want to pack it in now, I can't blame you.

11   INGRID. No, I don't want to pack it in. [*She lifts her face to be kissed.* VIC *fondles her for a moment then starts to unbutton her blouse.*] No, Vic.

12   VIC. What's wrong?

13   INGRID. Somebody might come.

14   VIC. You're not expecting anybody, are you?

15   INGRID. No, but you never know.

16   VIC. Lock the door.

17   INGRID. I already have.

18   VIC. Well, come on, Ingrid, come on.

19   INGRID. I . . . I can't undress while you're here.

20   VIC. I'll do it for you.

21   INGRID. No, I can't, Vic, honest. You'll have to go away.

22   VIC. Okay, then. [*He goes to door.*] I want to go to the bathroom anyway.

23   INGRID. Vic. [*He turns.*] You won't be rough with me, will you?

24   VIC. No, of course I won't. I promise.

25   INGRID. And we've got to be careful.

26   VIC. [*gently reassuring*]. Don't worry. It'll be okay.

46

1　INGRID. We've let the coffee get cold.

> VIC *smiles weakly and goes out.* INGRID *kicks off her shoes. She switches on the standard lamp and puts out the main light. She takes off her skirt and then her blouse. She is in waist-slip and bra. As she reaches behind to unfasten her bra, the scene ends.*

SCENE 14　　　THE RECORD SHOP

A record of Beethoven's Seventh is just ending.

2　MR. VAN HUYTEN. What do you think of that, then, Victor?

3　VIC. Great, just great. You know, there are some pieces like that, that kind of hit you straight in the guts, and others that are just plain hard to listen to.

4　MR. VAN HUYTEN. But often they're the most rewarding in the end. Great music endures for hundreds of years. It will be listened to as long as men live. You can't expect music of that stature to have the immediate appeal of a popular song. You must be patient, Victor, and let it work on you. One day, you'll hear the most wonderful music where you now hear only a din.

5　VIC. I certainly seem to find something new to like every week.

6　MR. VAN HUYTEN. There's all the music in the world just waiting for you to find it. I only wish I could go back fifty years and discover it all over again.

7　VIC [*impulsively*]. You know, Mr. Van Huyten, I think coming to work for you is the best thing I've ever done.

8　MR. VAN HUYTEN [*chuckles happily*]. Do you, Victor? I'm pleased to hear you say so. I'm glad to know you're happy with us.

9　VIC. I am, Mr. Van Huyten. I really am.

> *The* GIRL *we have seen before enters the shop.*

10　MR. VAN HUYTEN. Good morning. Can I help you?

11　GIRL. Have you got the Beatles' latest?

1 MR. VAN HUYTEN. I think this is your department, Victor.

2 VIC. Yes, I'll see to this. [*He reaches for the record.*] Here we are.

3 GIRL. Has that friend of yours been in lately?

4 VIC. Who, Willy? No, I haven't seen him for a couple of
      weeks. Did you go out with him that night?

5 GIRL. Are you kidding? Him and his father's car. The most
      he can borrow from his dad is an old push-bike. Can I
      listen to this?

   The phone rings and MR. VAN HUYTEN *answers it.*

6 VIC. Help yourself. I'll tell him you've been asking after
      him, shall I?

7 GIRL [*marching off to cubicle*]. Tell him what you like for me.
   VIC *laughs.*

8 MR. VAN HUYTEN. It's for you, Victor. [*He goes off into back of
      shop.*]

9 VIC. Oh, thanks. [*picks up phone*] Hello. Oh, hello, Ingrid. How's
      things? . . . Well, we've been busy, you know, stock-
      taking . . . No, I'll be here till late, I'm afraid. What?
      Are you sure? . . . It can't have . . . No, 'course it can't
      . . . Of course I'm sure . . . Yes, okay. Yes, tomorrow
      afternoon, Sunday, usual place. Yes, I'll be there. And
      look, don't get in a state about it. It'll be all right . . .
      About three, yes, I'll be there.

   VIC *puts phone down, looking worried. Without thinking he switches
   off the power in the cubicle and the Beatles whine to a halt. The*
   GIRL *sticks her head out.*

10 GIRL. Hey, me record's gone off.

11 VIC. What? Oh, sorry.

   He switches on the power again but the GIRL *brings the record out
   of the cubicle.*

12 GIRL. It doesn't matter. I've heard it before, actually. [*She
   hands record and ten-shilling note to* VIC.] I'll take it.

13 VIC. Thanks. I'll put it in a bag for you.

14 GIRL. I think they're fab, don't you?

1 VIC. Who?

2 GIRL. The Beatles.

3 VIC. Oh, Yes, they are. There you are. [*Hands her record and change.*]

4 GIRL. Ta. See you sometime. [*She goes to door then turns back.*] Here, you've given me too much. You've given me change for a pound instead of ten bob. [*She hands him ten-shilling note back.*]

5 VIC. Thanks. I was thinking about something else.

6 GIRL. You must be in love or something.

7 VIC [*thoughtfully*]. Or something.

SCENE 15   THE PARK
              Sunday afternoon

Distant sound of brass band. VIC *is walking about in front of* INGRID *who is sitting on the bench.*

8 VIC. Let's get it straight, then. It's a fortnight.

9 INGRID. Fifteen days.

10 VIC. Okay, fifteen days. It's not such a long time.

11 INGRID. It is with me.

12 VIC. Look, how can anything have gone wrong? How can it?

13 INGRID. You know very well it can.

14 VIC. But people try for ages sometimes before it comes off. I'm not even sure we . . .

15 INGRID. All I know is it's never happened before . . . I'm scared, Vic.

        VIC *himself is scared stiff but trying to hide it under a front of confidence.*

16 VIC. Maybe you're run down and need a tonic or something. Perhaps you should see the doctor.

17 INGRID. I've a feeling I shall be seeing the doctor before long, only it won't be for a tonic.

1 VIC. Whatever you do, don't get panicky. There's always a chance.

2 INGRID. There's something else. I didn't want to tell you over the phone . . . My mother knows.

3 VIC. What!

4 INGRID. I had to tell her.

5 VIC. Oh, for crying out loud, Ingrid, why did you have to do a daft thing like that? Couldn't you have kept quiet about it? I mean, suppose it's all a . . .

6 INGRID. I had to tell her. She knew something was wrong and she started asking me questions. You don't know what it's like. I had to tell her.

7 VIC. Oh, hell . . . that's done it. What did she say?

8 INGRID. I've never seen her so mad. I daren't tell you all she did say.

9 VIC. About me?

10 INGRID. What do you think?

11 VIC. What's she going to do now?

12 INGRID. She says she'll wait another week, then take me to the doctor's.

13 VIC. I suppose she'll want to see me then.

14 INGRID. She said she'd write for me dad to come home. She says you'll have a man to face when you do come.

VIC *walks to edge of stage and looks down the hill at the band.*

15 VIC. Listen to that band. Blasting away as if nothing had happened.

16 INGRID. Well, it's nothing to do with them, is it? You can't expect them to change the tune just because of us.

17 VIC. Oh, what a bloody awful mess.

18 INGRID. I suppose we should have thought about it before.

19 VIC [*indignantly*]. But it's a bit of bloody hard luck when you get caught first time.

20 INGRID [*with bitter humour*]. You'll have to write a letter to somebody about it.

A young couple go by, arms round each other, the girl giggling. VIC *eyes them sourly.*

1   VIC. I mean, if we'd been going at it hammer and tongs, having a helluva time.

2   INGRID. Vic, I'm scared. What are we going to do?

3   VIC. Do? There's only one thing we can do. We'll get married. [INGRID *begins to sob.*] Look, don't worry about it. I said we'll get married.

4   INGRID. I've always wanted to marry you, Vic. I used to imagine—at one time, anyway—how you might propose to me. And now it has to be like this. Forcing you into it. You'd never have asked me but for this, would you? I know you wouldn't.

5   VIC. I've asked you, haven't I? I've said we'll get married.

6   INGRID. You've no need to if you don't want. I shan't force you.

7   VIC [*wryly*]. No, but you won't turn me down, will you?

8   INGRID [*crying again*]. I won't. I've always wanted you. You know I have.

9   VIC [*sombrely*]. Well, now you've got me.

    CURTAIN

Act 2

MRS. BROWN *is ironing.* ARTHUR *is sitting at the table, among the teapots, doing his football pools.* VIC *is supposed to be eating his tea but he has no appetite.*

1 MRS. BROWN. You're not getting your tea, Victor.

2 VIC. I don't feel up to it today.

3 MRS. BROWN. You reckon to be fond of finny haddock, don't you?

4 VIC. I like it all right. I'm just not hungry, that's all.

5 MRS. BROWN. You haven't been filling yourself with all sorts of pegmeg this afternoon, have you?

6 VIC. No, I haven't had a thing.

VIC pokes about on his plate and ARTHUR *mutters to himself as he fills in his pools coupon.*

7 ARTHUR. What do you think about Sheffield United? [VIC *does not hear him.*] I'm talking to you, Vic.

8 VIC. What?

9 ARTHUR. I said what do you think about Sheffield United this week?

10 VIC. How the heck should I know? They don't call me Old Moore.

11 ARTHUR. 'Ere, 'ere. I asked you a civil question, young feller.

12 VIC. Well I don't know everything about football. Why don't you use your own judgment instead of keep asking me?

ARTHUR *lifts his eyebrows and looks at* MRS. BROWN.

13 MRS. BROWN. Have you been having some sort o' trouble at the shop, Victor?

14 VIC. I'm all right. [*He gets up and takes evening paper. He sits down in*

*fireside chair and pretends to read. After a pause he speaks from
behind the paper.*] I'm thinking of getting married.

They both gape at him, MRS. BROWN *dropping the iron on to its
stand with a clatter.*

2 MRS. BROWN. Who are you thinking o' marrying?

3 VIC. A lass called Ingrid Rothwell. She lives up on Park
Drive.

4 MRS. BROWN. How is it we haven't heard owt of it before?

5 VIC. I didn't know before. I've only just made me mind up.

6 MRS. BROWN. It's happen a case of you've *had* to make your
mind up, is it? [VIC *lowers the newspaper and looks uncomfortable.*]
Is it a forced do, Victor? [VIC *gives an awkward little shrug
and* MRS. BROWN, *losing her temper, tears the paper out of his
hands and stands over him.*] You fool. You gret silly fool.
You with all your future afore you, getting yerself
entangled with some cheap young piece 'at knows
nowt but carrying on and getting down on her—

7 VIC. She's not like that. How can you call her when you
don't even know her?

8 MRS. BROWN. I know this much about her. She's trapped you
nicely. When I think of all the decent respectable lasses
you could ha' married and you come home and tell
us you're wedding some little slut 'at's got her claws
into you this way—

VIC *jumps up and shouts.*

9 VIC. She's not like that, I tell you. You don't even know her

ARTHUR *gets up and comes between them.*

10 ARTHUR. Nah, just a minute, you two. It's allus been my
experience 'at there's two folk to reckon with in cases
like this.

11 MRS. BROWN. Your experience? What do you know about it?

12 ARTHUR. Well I'm sixty-one year old, and I courted thee
and married thee and helped thee bring a family into
t'world, so I reckon I know a bit . . . Now fair's fair and
I don't like to hear you carrying on about this lass

before you've even met her. I don't know who's most to blame but it's bound to be a bit o' both. Our Victor's only yuman like any young feller and if this lass is a bit soft-hearted and affectionate like, then summat like this can happen. It's not t'first time and it won't be t'last. An' if our Victor's had his fun he's a right to pay for it just like anybody else.

2   MRS. BROWN. How old is she?

3   VIC. Nineteen

4   ARTHUR. Nobbut a bairn.

5   MRS. BROWN. There's many a lass at her age 'at can tell me a thing or two.

6   ARTHUR. An' happen she's not one of 'em or she might not have got into this. Have you seen her parents, Victor?

7   VIC. I'm going tonight. I wanted to tell you first.

8   MRS. BROWN. Very thoughtful, I must say. Well you just watch your manners. We don't want 'em thinking you come from any sort of family.

9   ARTHUR. An' when are you thinking of bringing her here?

10 VIC. I reckon it can be any time now.

11 MRS. BROWN. I'm not so sure I want her in my house.

12 ARTHUR. Talk a bit o' sense, Lucy. You can't turn your own daughter-in-law away.

13 MRS. BROWN. She's not me daughter-in-law yet.

14 ARTHUR. If you ask me, the quicker she is, the better for everybody.

The lights fade

SCENE 2   THE ROTHWELLS' LIVING-ROOM

MR. ROTHWELL *is in shirtsleeves reading the newspaper when door chimes are heard. He looks at his watch.*

15 MR. ROTHWELL [*calls*]. Ingrid!

16 INGRID [*off*]. What is it?

1 MR. ROTHWELL. Come and answer the door, will you? [INGRID *appears from her bedroom.*] Let him in while I go and put my jacket on.

  MR. ROTHWELL *goes off while* INGRID *answers door and lets* VIC *in.*

2 VIC. Hello.

3 INGRID. Hello. Come in. [*She leads* VIC *into living-room.*]

4 VIC. Where are they?

5 INGRID. They'll be in in a minute.

6 VIC. How're you feeling?

7 INGRID. I've been a bit queasy, but I'm not too bad. Did you tell them?

8 VIC. Yes, I told 'em.

9 INGRID. What did they say?

10 VIC. What didn't they say? I thought me mother was going to clout me with the iron. The Old Man was reasonable enough, though.

11 INGRID. I don't know how I'm ever going to face them.

12 VIC. Oh, you'll be okay. They'll see straight away that you're a decent girl.

13 INGRID. Is that what you told them—that I'm a decent girl?

14 VIC. Well you are, aren't you? You know I've always thought so. [INGRID *is near to tears.*] Now what's wrong?

15 INGRID. It's nothing . . . It's just when you're nice to me.

16 VIC [*awkwardly*]. Come on, cheer up.

17 INGRID. Vic, they'll be coming in in a minute. Remember to act as if you've never been in the house before.

18 VIC. You didn't tell them about that, then?

19 INGRID. No.

20 VIC. But where do they think—?

21 INGRID. In the park.

22 VIC. Oh Lord.

23 INGRID. I just couldn't say here.

24 VIC. Well, if you think so . . .

MR. ROTHWELL *comes in.*

1 MR. ROTHWELL. Nippy out tonight, is it? Turning colder again. Well, you'd better sit down, young man. Take his coat, Ingrid, make yourself useful. You might like to pop and see where your mother is while I have a chat with, er, Victor. [INGRID *does as she is told and there is an awkward pause between* VIC *and* MR. ROTHWELL. *The latter offers cigarettes.*] Do you smoke?

2 VIC. Oh, yes . . . thanks.

3 MR. ROTHWELL. I don't suppose you've been looking forward to this?

4 VIC. Can't say I have. Had to face it, though.

5 MR. ROTHWELL. Right enough. I like a man who faces his responsibilities. Ingrid's told us you've asked her to marry you.

6 VIC. Oh, yes . . . well, I mean, I did straight away when I . . . when she . . .

7 MR. ROTHWELL. It came as a bit of a shock to you, did it?

8 VIC. I'll say it did.

9 MR. ROTHWELL. You must have known it might happen, though.

10 VIC. Well, I suppose I knew it was possible. But it wasn't as if we'd . . . [*He can't find the words.*]

11 MR. ROTHWELL. Made a habit of it, you mean?

12 VIC. Well, yes.

13 MR. ROTHWELL. You've told your parents, of course?

14 VIC. Yes, I told them tonight.

15 MR. ROTHWELL. How did they take it?

16 VIC. They were a bit upset. Me father seemed a lot calmer than me mother.

17 MR. ROTHWELL. Yes, I expect so. Women are a lot more emotional about these things. It's their nature, I suppose. A man's too busy thinking about what's to be done. Ingrid tells me you were a draughtsman at Whittaker's before you went into the shop. I was a bit

surprised to hear you'd given up a good trade like draughtsmanship to be a shop assistant.

2 VIC. Oh, I thought about all that before I decided. You see, Mr. Van Huyten's a friend of the family, like, and that makes it a bit different.

3 MR. ROTHWELL. I see.

4 VIC. Well, I mean he depends on me a lot, and we get on well together. I like working there.

5 MR. ROTHWELL. It's worth a lot. Are the prospects good?

6 VIC. I think so. I'm more or less my own boss now, with Mr. Van Huyten getting on a bit. He's handing over more and more responsibility to me and the business is building up.

7 MR. ROTHWELL. It sounds promising, I must say. This Mr. Van Huyten must like you.

8 VIC. Well, we get on well.

MRS. ROTHWELL *comes in with* INGRID. *Both she and* MR. ROTH-WELL *are in their forties and much younger than* VIC's *parents. On the face of it they look sharper, brighter, but while* MR. ROTH-WELL *is an amiable and reasonable man,* MRS. ROTHWELL *is a narrow, small-town snob and this situation, in which she has a genuine grievance, brings out the worst in her.*

9 MR. ROTHWELL. Oh, here they are.

10 INGRID. Mother, this is Vic.

11 VIC. Er, good evening. [*He stands up and half extends his hand then lets it drop. His nervousness in the face of* MRS. ROTHWELL's *stony expression causes him to smile foolishly and babble.*] I'm sorry we have to meet in circumstances like these.

12 MRS. ROTHWELL. It's a bit late to think about that, isn't it? How long have you known Ingrid?

13 VIC. We've been friendly for about six months now.

14 MRS. ROTHWELL. Friendly! I suppose you know that this business has upset Ingrid's father and I very much.

15 VIC. I suppose it must have. It's only natural

16 MRS. ROTHWELL. I expect your parents have had something to say about it as well?

1 VIC. Oh, yes, well, I mean . . .

2 MRS. ROTHWELL. And I suppose they're trying to pin all the blame on Ingrid, saying she enticed you into it.

3 VIC. Oh, no. I wouldn't say that.

4 MRS. ROTHWELL. Well I'll have you know that we think there's very little blame on Ingrid's side at all. I know the way I've brought my daughter up and I know what sort of girl she is. She'd only do a thing like that under extreme persuasion. We've always had high hopes of the match she'd make and we don't like having the pistol levelled at our heads like this.

5 MR. ROTHWELL. Yes, yes, Esther, that's all very well but we can't do anything about it now. I think we ought to be getting down to practical matters, such as how soon they can be married and where they're going to live.

6 MRS. ROTHWELL. I just want to make it clear that this sort of thing involves other people besides the two of them.

7 MR. ROTHWELL. Yes, Esther, I'm sure Victor appreciates that. I think he's as sorry about this now as any young man could be. I don't like the idea of young people starting married life like this any more than anybody else does, but the damage is done now and we shall just have to make the best of it. Now, about the wedding. I should say in three or four weeks' time at the latest, and quietly, without fuss. What do you think, Victor?

8 VIC [*feebly*]. Well, yes, any time really.

9 MRS. ROTHWELL. When I think of the nice wedding I've always imagined for Ingrid. All in white, at the church, with the choir and all our relatives and friends there . . .

10 INGRID. It doesn't matter, Mother. I don't mind.

11 MRS. ROTHWELL. But *I* do. It's a mother's proudest day.

12 MR. ROTHWELL. Well, I'm afraid there's nothing we can do about that now so we shall just have to put it out of our minds. The next thing is where they're going to live. Have you got any ideas about that, Victor?

1 VIC. I don't know, really. I suppose we could live at our
   house for a while. We don't stand a chance of finding a
   house of our own for a bit.

2 MR. ROTHWELL. What do your parents think of that idea?

3 VIC. I haven't actually mentioned it yet. I don't think they'd
   mind, though.

4 MR. ROTHWELL. Well I have a suggestion. We talked it over
   before you came. I'm away a lot of the time and if
   Ingrid leaves too it means her mother will be on her
   own. Of course, Ingrid can't stay at home to keep her
   mother company for ever, but for the present there's
   no reason why you shouldn't live here. It'll give you a
   breathing space. Well, what d'you think?

5 VIC [*a moment's pause*]. All right . . . Thank you. It's very kind of
   you.

6 MR. ROTHWELL. That's that, then. We'll stop crying over
   spilt milk. [*He crosses to the cupboard.*] Well, I don't know
   about you but I could do with a drink after that.
   Esther?

7 MRS. ROTHWELL. No, thanks. And you'd better not either,
   Ingrid.

8 MR. ROTHWELL. What about you, Victor?

9 VIC. Thanks. Just a small one, please.

10 MR. ROTHWELL. There's not a large selection. Scotch all right?

11 VIC. Yes, thanks.

   MR. ROTHWELL *hands* VIC *a drink.*

12 MR. ROTHWELL. I'm sure things will work out all right if we
   give them a chance. From what Ingrid's told me I
   think she'd like nothing better than to be Vic's wife,
   baby or no baby. I didn't know what to think before
   I met you but now I have I feel a lot better about it.
   I think we shall all get on together, don't you?

13 VIC. Er, yes. [*He looks at* MRS. ROTHWELL *whose face is like flint.*]
   Cheers.

SCENE 3   A STREET CORNER

VIC *and* WILLY *stand talking.*

1 VIC. Will you be up there again next Wednesday, Willy?
2 WILLY. We're always there Wednesday nights.
3 VIC. Have to see if I can manage it, then.
4 WILLY. Depends whether the old ball and chain's on, eh?
5 VIC. You've got somebody else to think about, y'know, when you're married.
6 WILLY. That's why I'm not joining.
7 VIC. It happens to most people, sooner or later.
8 WILLY. With me it'll be later. You know, all I could think of when I was coming out of the registry office with you was how fast you sign yourself away. There was a bird going by as we got to the gate. I noticed she'd got nice legs and stiletto heels and then all at once it struck me that you'd never be able to look at a bird with an open mind again. Married. Forty years, mebbe. a real life sentence, with no time off for good behaviour, and a mother-in-law thrown in as a bonus.
9 VIC. Aw, she's not so bad. Her and Ingrid get on well, and we shan't be living there forever.
10 WILLY. What about the old feller?
11 VIC. Oh, *he's* all right. He's just not at home much.
12 WILLY. That leaves you between the two of 'em, eh?
13 VIC. Oh, belt up, Willy. You don't know owt about it.
14 WILLY. What did I say? [*He wanders off with a wave.*] See you next week, then, all being well. Give my regards to the family. [*Goes off leaving* VIC *looking disgruntled.*]

SCENE 4   THE ROTHWELLS' LIVING-ROOM
Night

VIC, INGRID *and* MRS. ROTHWELL, *who is already knitting for the baby.*

1   MRS. ROTHWELL. . . . and of course I never got to the hair-dresser's at all because I was waiting all day for the coal merchant to deliver and he hasn't been yet. You can't rely on anybody nowadays.

2   VIC. Couldn't you go out and let them deliver when they can?

3   MRS. ROTHWELL. How do I know what they're doing if I'm not here to watch them? I know all their tricks, you know. Putting five bags into the cellar and getting you to sign for six.

4   VIC. I suppose it does happen sometimes.

5   MRS. ROTHWELL. And the price of coal just goes up and up, what with the way the miners behave. No sense of responsibility. Higher and higher wages. Thirty and forty pounds a week and it isn't as if it's hard work any more with all this mechanization. Money poured into the mines to make it easier for them and all they do in return is force up the price of coal.

6   VIC. That just isn't true.

7   MRS. ROTHWELL. What do you mean?

8   VIC. My father's a miner and he doesn't get anything like forty quid a week. And anybody who thinks there's no more shovelling and hard work in a pit wants to go down and have a look.

9   MRS. ROTHWELL [*ignoring the argument*]. The country's been going down ever since the war and it won't take many more years before we touch rock bottom. What with Englishmen without responsibility and now all these coloured people coming in for a life on relief . . .

VIC *gives up and changes the subject.*

61

1 VIC. Mr. Van Huyten was asking me today if we'd like to go to a concert in Leeds with him, Ingrid.

2 INGRID. A symphoney concert?

3 VIC. Yeh. It's the London Symphony. You don't often get a chance to hear 'em in the flesh.

4 INGRID. I'd be bored to tears.

5 VIC. Why don't you give it a try? There's always a first time.

6 MRS. ROTHWELL. Ingrid knows what she likes and she doesn't have to pretend to enjoy highbrow nonsense.

7 VIC. Who's pretending?

8 MRS. ROTHWELL. Lots of people pretend because they think it makes them superior.

9 VIC. Mebbe they do. Makes a change from television quiz shows, anyway. What about it, Ingrid?

10 INGRID. I just don't think it's in my line, Vic.

11 VIC. It's a long time since I heard a good concert.

12 INGRID. I just know I wouldn't like it.

13 VIC. Well I'd like to go anyway.

14 MRS. ROTHWELL. You have to sacrifice when you're married. Give and take.

15 VIC. I don't see what me going to a concert's got to do with it.

16 MRS. ROTHWELL. If you want to carry on just as you did before you were married it's got nothing to do with me. But I'm sure Ingrid will have something to say about it. [*She stands up.*] Well, I don't know about you two, but I'm going to bed. [*goes to door*] You'll just wash up those few things before you go, won't you, Ingrid?

17 INGRID. Yes, all right. Goodnight, Mother.

18 MRS. ROTHWELL. Goodnight. Goodnight, Victor.

19 VICTOR. Goodnight. [MRS. ROTHWELL *goes out.*] What about it, then?

20 INGRID. What?

21 VIC. The concert.

22 INGRID. When is it?

1 VIC. A week on Saturday.

2 INGRID. We might want to go somewhere else.

3 VIC. Aye, anywhere but to a concert. I don't know what's coming over you, Ingrid. You're just an echo of your mother. She was even interfering on our honeymoon.

4 INGRID. She was only thinking about me.

5 VIC. A fine thing! Filling yer full of ideas about being careful. Trying to turn you frigid on our wedding night. Whoever said mothers-in-law were a joke!

6 INGRID. You should show a bit of respect for her, Vic. After all, we are living in her house.

7 VIC. Don't I know it!

8 INGRID. Are you going, then?

9 VIC. Yes, I am.

10 INGRID. You're going to make an issue of it?

11 VIC. *Me? I'm* making an issue of it? You let your mother drive me into a corner and then say I'm making an issue of it. Just because you can't think of anything but watching bloody television till your eyes drop out.

12 INGRID. For goodness' sake keep your voice down. She can hear every word.

13 VIC [*louder*]. I don't care what she can hear. She'll hear a lot more before I've done.

MRS. ROTHWELL *comes back in.*

14 MRS. ROTHWELL. If you two want to sit up talking till all hours you might at least do it quietly. [*She appears to be addressing both of them but she looks directly at* VIC *as she finishes.*]

15 INGRID. I'm sorry, Mother. We'll be coming to bed in a minute. [MRS. ROTHWELL *goes out.*] Look, Vic, I don't want you to think you can't do anything on your own any more.

16 VIC. Oh! Thanks very much! You want to tell her that sometime. If I set me mind on going to this concert neither you nor your mother will stop me. But I'm all for a quiet life and as I've got to live here I'll give it a

miss. I'll tell you straight, though—I didn't bargain for this bloody lot when I married you.

2 INGRID. There's no need to swear. You're always swearing these days.

3 VIC. This lot's enough to make a parson swear.

4 INGRID. You go if you want to. [*She starts collecting the supper things together.*]

5 VIC. And get the big-freeze treatment for it? No thanks. I haven't forgotten Conroy's party.

6 INGRID. Well, you went to that, didn't you?

7 VIC. And paid for it.

8 INGRID. It's up to you.

9 VIC. Aye, it's up to me. You never back me up, do you? You let your mother say just what she likes and you never think of siding with me, do you?

10 INGRID. I don't see why I should fall out with her. I never used to and I won't start now.

11 VIC. Not even to save my face, eh?

12 INGRID. She's my mother, Vic.

13 VIC. Yes, and I'm your husband. I know anybody 'ud take me for the lodger, but I remember signing me name all right.

INGRID *is at the door with the pots.* VIC *opens it for her.*

14 INGRID. Perhaps you're sorry you married me. [*She goes out on this and* VIC *turns back into the room.*]

15 VIC. There's no bloody perhaps about it.

SCENE 5   THE RECORD SHOP
            A quiet afternoon

MR. VAN HUYTEN *is working on the accounts.* VIC *is prowling about checking stock with sheet of paper and pencil.*

16 VIC. Do you realize, Mr. Van Huyten, we've sold twenty-

two of those little transistors? I told you it'd be worth
trying them.

2   MR. VAN HUYTEN [*twinkles*]. Are you speaking as a shopkeeper
or a music lover?

3   VIC. Oh, I know the quality's not all that great but it's good
business and they do play music. [*He grins.*] They get
the pop programme a treat.

4   MR. VAN HUYTEN. Well, from Beat to Beethoven, it's not all
that long a step.

5   VIC. Not with a bit of encouragement. [*He pauses in what he is
doing.*] I must say we could do with a bit now. It's quiet.

6   MR. VAN HUYTEN. It always is on Monday afternoons. It
gives you a chance to catch up on the paperwork.
Here's somebody now. Your next-door neighbour,
isn't it?

7   VIC. Oh yes. You can rely on her. [*Door opens and* MRS. OLI-
PHANT *comes in.*] Hello, Mrs. Oliphant. Come to pay
your dues and demands?

8   MRS. OLIPHANT. Hello, Victor.

*She has spoken as though surprised to see him and as she hands over
hire-purchase account book she looks at him in a way that makes him
ask:*

9   VIC. Is there something wrong?

10   MRS. OLIPHANT. I didn't expect to see you here. I thought
you'd be up at the hospital.

11   VIC. Hospital?

12   MRS. OLIPHANT. Didn't you know? But surely . . . It's Ingrid.
She's had an accident. [VIC *is shaking his head in puzzlement.*]
She fell downstairs and hurt herself.

13   VIC. How do you mean?

14   MRS. OLIPHANT. It was just this afternoon. They've taken
her into hospital. You mean to say you didn't know?

15   VIC. No, I didn't know a thing about it. Is she bad?

16   MRS. OLIPHANT. I don't really know. She looked poorly.
It's the baby, you see. I think she brought on a miscarriage.

1 VIC. Is it the Infirmary they've taken her to?

2 MRS. OLIPHANT. Ooh, now, let me think ... No, it was the General. Yes, that's right. I remember somebody saying.

3 MR. VAN HUYTEN. Shall I telephone for you, Victor?

4 VIC. Yes ... please.

5 MRS. OLIPHANT. I should have thought Ingrid's mother would phone you straight away. I mean, it's sometime ago now.

6 VIC. No, I don't know anything about it.

7 MR. VAN HUYTEN [*on phone*]. General Hospital? One moment, please ... Victor, I've got them.

8 VIC. Oh, thanks. Thanks very much. [*takes phone and speaks into it*] Hello ... I'm enquiring about a Mrs. Brown. She was brought in this afternoon. She had an accident, a miscarriage, early this afternoon ... What? This is Mr. Brown. My name's Victor Brown, hers is Ingrid ... Yes, all right. [*pause,* VIC *looks round from phone*] She's finding out ... Hello, yes? ... I see. When will you know? ... Yes, I'll do that. I'll come up. Thank you. [*puts phone down*] Probably wondering why I'm not there already.

9 MRS. OLIPHANT. No news?

10 VIC. No.

11 MRS. OLIPHANT. I'm sure she'll be all right. I had a miscarriage once and I didn't even go away. I've had both my children since then, so you can see it didn't do me any harm. And Ingrid wasn't very far gone, was she?

12 VIC. No, not far ... I ... I think I'll get up there.

13 MR. VAN HUYTEN. Yes, off you go, Victor. I'll see to things here. I hope you find everything all right.

VIC *gets his coat and goes out. They stand looking after him.*

14 MRS. OLIPHANT. I can't understand it. You'd think she'd have let him know straight away.

SCENE 6   THE HOSPITAL CORRIDOR OR WAITING HALL

VIC *comes on.* A WOMAN DOCTOR, *in white coat, appears.*

1   DR. PARKER. Can I help you?

2   VIC. The nurse told me to wait here. I was looking for Mrs. Brown. Ingrid Brown.

3   DR. PARKER. You're Mr. Brown? [VIC *nods.*] I'm Dr. Parker. I've just left your wife.

4   VIC. How is she?

5   DR. PARKER. As well as can be expected. She's had a very uncomfortable afternoon, but she's going to be all right. I'm sorry about the baby. I'm afraid we couldn't save it.

6   VIC. No ...

7   DR. PARKER. Have you been married long?

8   VIC. Three months, a bit more.

9   DR. PARKER. I see.

10   VIC. She was having the baby before.

11   DR. PARKER. I see. Well, you'll have other children, all being well.

12   VIC. Can I see her?

13   DR. PARKER. I'd rather you didn't at the moment. I'd like her to get some sleep. Her mother's just leaving her now. A rather emotional person. If you'd come earlier, in the afternoon.

14   VIC. I didn't know.

15   DR. PARKER. I believe your wife's mother was with her. Didn't she let you know?

16   VIC. A neighbour told me. I'd be the last one she'd think of telling ... Anyway, will you tell her I've been and I came as soon as I knew?

17   DR. PARKER. Yes, I'll tell her. Is there anything else?

18   VIC. You can tell her not to bother about the kid on my

account. I couldn't get used to the idea of being a
father anyway.

2 DR. PARKER. Here's your mother-in-law now.

MRS. ROTHWELL *comes on.*

3 VIC. How is she?

4 MRS ROTHWELL. How do you expect? I wish she'd never laid
eyes on you.

She walks on.

SCENE 7   THE ROTHWELLS' LIVING-ROOM

INGRID *is doing her hair in the mirror. As she has her arms raised* VIC *embraces her from behind. She struggles and protests.*

5 INGRID. Can't you see I'm doing my hair?

6 VIC. I can see you don't want me to touch you.

7 INGRID. I don't know what you mean.

8 VIC. How long is all this going on? That's what I want to
know. You'll have to snap out of it sometime, you know.

9 INGRID. What do you mean 'snap out of it'?

10 VIC. What I say. You can't act up on the strength of your
miscarriage for ever.

11 INGRID. So you think I'm just putting on an act, do you?

12 VIC. Mebbe you don't know it. Your mother'll have you
thinking you're poorly for the rest of your life. But
I'm getting a bit fed up of it.

13 INGRID. Always thinking of yourself.

14 VIC. Look, it's three months since the accident. It's time I
could make a pass at you without feeling like a dirty
old man.

15 INGRID. If that's all you can think of you'll just have to
show a bit of will power.

16 VIC. Till when? Till your mother gives the word? If she
wants to split us up she's going the right way about it.

It took some doing for me to come back after you had your accident, the way she treated me.

2　INGRID. Why did you come back, then?

3　VIC. Because we're married, and you'd got a plateful of trouble without me adding to it by walking out.

4　INGRID. I'm glad you can remember who did the suffering. I was the one who went through it, you know.

5　VIC. You think I didn't care? I walked out of that hospital and I was physically sick. I went into a public lavatory and retched my guts up.

6　INGRID. I don't have to thank you for feeling like any normal husband, do I?

7　VIC. How the hell do I get you to act like a normal wife, that's what I want to know. Well I'll tell you straight, I was all for making the best of it, but if we're married we're married and I'm not going to be the lodger.

The door opens and MRS. ROTHWELL *comes in in her outdoor clothes and with a large coatbox under her arm.*

8　MRS. ROTHWELL. Ingrid, I—

9　VIC. Would you mind not barging in when we're talking?

10　MRS. ROTHWELL. Talking, you call it! More like shouting. I could hear you before I opened the front door . . . I was going to say, Ingrid, I've got the coat. They've altered it beautifully. [*She opens box and takes out coat and holds it up.*] I should just slip it on and try it.

11　VIC. Coat! She doesn't need any coat. She's got a bloody wardrobe full. How the hell can we save up and get out of here if she's spending it all on coats?

12　INGRID. I'll thank you not to speak to my mother like that.

13　VIC. Are we going out or aren't we?

14　INGRID. I'm not going anywhere while you're in that mood.

15　VIC. All right, then, stop in and wear your bloody coat.

He snatches the coat from MRS. ROTHWELL *and slings it across at* INGRID *who bursts into tears. He slams out.*

VIC *and* WILLY *come on from side, holding on to each other, both of them drunk.*

1　WILLY. Here we are, then, home sweet home.

2　VIC. That's a laugh.

3　WILLY. Are you all right?

4　VIC. I'm drunk, Willy. I went out to get drunk and I have achieved that object. And you, Willy, my dear old pal, are a friend close to my heart who listens to my tale of woe and brings me comfort in my hour of need.

　　The lights come up to show MRS. ROTHWELL, *in dressing-gown, sitting in her living-room.*

5　WILLY. This is as far as I go, though, mate. You're on your own from here. And there's a light on so somebody must be waiting for you.

6　VIC. It'll be the Queen Mother. She'll be sitting—and knitting—with a martyred look on her silly face. [*He giggles.*]

7　WILLY. You're sure you're okay?

8　VIC. I can handle this, Willy. Leave that to me. Let there be one single word out of place and see what happens. Just see what happens.

9　WILLY. Go on, then. I'll give you a tinkle at the shop.

10　VIC. You do that, Willy. And we'll go and get drunk again.

11　WILLY. So long, then. [*He goes off.*]

12　VIC. So long, Willy. Farewell, dear old pal.

　　VIC *wanders away behind the bungalow set singing 'Dear old pals, jolly old pals . . .' and rings the door chimes.* MRS. ROTHWELL *stands up and picks up the little clock off the mantelshelf.* VIC *now raps in a tattoo on the door.* MRS. ROTHWELL, *still holding the clock, goes and lets him in.*

13　VIC. Oh, is Ingrid in bed, then?

1 MRS. ROTHWELL. She is. And I should have been as well if I
hadn't had to wait up for you. [*They come into room.*] Do
you know what time it is?

The confrontation with MRS. ROTHWELL *has sobered* VIC *up a
little.*

2 VIC. Let me guess. [*He peers at the clock in* MRS. ROTHWELL's *hand.*]
Twelve o'clock?

3 MRS. ROTHWELL. Yes, twelve o'clock, and people being kept
from their beds till you decide to come home.

VIC *takes his raincoat off and slings it over a chair.*

4 VIC. Home? You don't call this my home. Why I haven't
even got a key. I'm worse than a lodger.

5 MRS. ROTHWELL. I expect people who live in my house to
accept my standards. You can do as you like when
you're in a home of your own.

6 VIC. The way things are going we'll be here for the next
twenty years. It's about time Ingrid got back to work.

7 MRS. ROTHWELL. I don't know that Ingrid wants to go back
to work. She thinks like me—that a husband who can't
support a wife is a poor fish.

8 VIC. Well she'll have to get rid of her fancy ideas. I'm no
mill-owner's son. Maybe that's what you had in mind
for her, eh? Somebody to keep her in luxury all the
rest of her life.

9 MRS. ROTHWELL. *You're* certainly not what I had in mind.

10 VIC. Well *I* married her. And bloody glad she was to have
me.

11 MRS. ROTHWELL. Is there any need for language like that?

12 VIC. Eh?

13 MRS. ROTHWELL. You swore.

14 VIC. I feel like swearing. I've felt like it ever since tea-time.

15 MRS. ROTHWELL. Well don't bring it here. Save it for your
friends.

16 VIC. *My* friends? You think your friends are the last word.
Such a nice class of people. Well let me tell you I've

been talking to a bloke tonight who's got more money than all *your* precious friends put together.

2　MRS. ROTHWELL. It seems he's been spending some of it on drink.

3　VIC. I've had a drink. I'm not denying it.

4　MRS. ROTHWELL. A drink? More like a dozen.

5　VIC. All right, then, I've had a dozen. Is there any law against it?

6　MRS. ROTHWELL. There's an elementary sense of decency that stops a man coming home to his wife in such a condition.

7　VIC. So I've no sense of decency now. I'd enough to marry your Ingrid when she was in trouble. And don't think she wasn't getting what she wanted. She'd have married me any time, baby or no baby.

8　MRS. ROTHWELL. She'd have been in a position to listen to advice if she hadn't been seduced.

9　VIC. That's a good 'un, that is. D'you think I had to tie her down to do it? If it hadn't been me it'd have been somebody else.

10　MRS. ROTHWELL [*finally losing her composure*]. How dare you make such disgusting accusations against my daughter's character! You walk in here, drunk, at this time of night, just as though you own the place, and sully a good girl's name with your filthy talk.

11　VIC. I feel sick.

12　MRS. ROTHWELL. I don't wonder, either. You'd better get— [*It is too late.* VIC *reels away and bends over the back of the sofa and vomits. For a moment* MRS. ROTHWELL *is speechless.*] You filthy disgusting pig. You're filth, nothing but filth.

VIC *starts to laugh. He laughs uncontrollably for a few moments as* MRS. ROTHWELL *slams out. Then all at once the situation is no longer funny. He gets some newspaper and cleans up behind the couch, throwing the paper on the fire. He lights a cigarette which he finds tastes foul to him. He throws it away and goes into passage and through door of his bedroom. He comes straight out again.*

1 VIC. Ingrid, where are you? [*He knocks on door of* MRS. ROTHWELL'S *room.*] Ingrid, are you in there?

2 MRS. ROTHWELL. Go away.

3 VIC. I want Ingrid.

4 MRS. ROTHWELL. She's not going to sleep with a drunken sot like you.

5 VIC. She's not what? [*He bangs on door.*] Send her out. D'you hear? I said send her out.

6 INGRID. Go to bed, Vic.

7 VIC. You come on into our room, where you belong.

8 INGRID. I'm staying in here tonight.

9 VIC. I'll come in and fetch you if you don't come out.

10 INGRID. The door's locked.

VIC *rattles the handle.*

11 VIC. What the hell are you playing at? [*thumps again*]

12 INGRID. Vic, go away. You'll wake the neighbours.

13 VIC. To hell with the neighbours. Now you come out.

14 MRS. ROTHWELL. For the last time, she's not leaving this room tonight.

15 VIC. All right, then, you old cow; you've done it. I know where I stand now. [*He marches back into his room and re-appears with a suitcase and a pile of clothes which he stuffs into the case. He puts on his raincoat and picks up the case. He stops for one last shout.*] You heard me, did you? I said I know where I stand now.

He walks out into the night.

SCENE 9   CHRISTINE'S FLAT

VIC, *in raincoat, is holding and looking at wedding photo of* CHRIS *and* DAVID. *He puts it down in wrong place as* CHRIS, *in dressing-gown, enters with tea and cups on a tray. She pours a cup for* VIC. *He takes the tea and gulps it as fast as its heat will allow.*

16 CHRIS. Don't scald your mouth.

73

1   VIC. God, that tastes good, though.

2   CHRIS [*refilling his cup*]. Well, come on, then, out with it. Is it you and Ingrid?

3   VIC. Yes. I've left her.

4   CHRIS. What brought this on?

5   VIC. That bloody woman. And Ingrid's right under her thumb. We had a few words last night and I went out and got plastered. When I got home Ingrid's mother was waiting for me and I told her a few things I'd been saving up. She took Ingrid into her room with her so I shoved a few things into a case and walked out.

6   CHRIS. And where have you been all night?

7   VIC. I dunno. Walking the streets.

8   CHRIS. You'd better take your coat off. [*He does so, dropping it on a chair.*] How long have things been like this?

9   VIC. Oh, it's been brewing up for ages.

10   CHRIS. Was it Ingrid losing the baby?

11   VIC. Not altogether. That just made it worse. I never really got on with Ingrid's mother. I was never good enough for her lovey-dovey daughter. You've seen her. You know what she's like. Do you know she never rang me when Ingrid fell? The woman next door told me when she came into the shop. Hours afterwards, it was. That's a fine thing, isn't it? And then she acted as if it was all my fault. Well I told her, I might not be good enough for her daughter but I did marry her when she was in trouble.

12   CHRIS. You *got* her into trouble, Vic.

13   VIC. I know. And I wish to God I hadn't. Oh, Chris, if only I could have met somebody like you, somebody to make me better than I am, not worse.

14   CHRIS. But you did marry Ingrid, didn't you? You did choose to marry her.

15   VIC. Aye. You've had your fun and now you can pay for it. What kind of choosing is that? You know there's only one thing to do round here when you put a girl in the

family way, and that's marry her. It doesn't matter whether you love her or not as long as you make her respectable.

CHRIS *picks up the photograph.*

2 CHRIS. But there must have been something, Vic.

She moves photo to its proper place. VIC *waves at it.*

3 VIC. Everybody's not like you and David, y'know. I thought it was like that with me and Ingrid at first, but it didn't last long.

4 CHRIS. Wasn't it rather selfish to go on seeing her if you knew that?

5 VIC. I suppose it was. Oh, I argued with meself about it. But she wanted me so I thought I might as well carry on. One night I went a bit too far and now I'm paying for it. It's worked out bloody expensive, Chris, I can tell you.

6 CHRIS. I see. [*sighs*] Well, you've made your own bed, haven't you?

7 VIC [*surprised*]. You say that? That's what everybody else'll say. Can't you say anything else?

8 CHRIS. It's no more than the truth, Vic.

9 VIC. I expected something different from you.

10 CHRIS. I'm trying to be honest with you. You've only yourself to blame. If you hadn't played about with this girl you wouldn't be here like this now. You're married and you can't just dismiss the fact.

11 VIC. I'm married, all right. You all made sure of that. You all stood around, pushing. There wasn't one of you who said no, don't do it if you don't want to.

12 CHRIS. You pushed yourself when you did what you did with Ingrid. At least you faced your responsibilities.

13 VIC. I don't know what to say, Chris. I could always talk to you. We seemed closer. You could always understand better than they could.

14 CHRIS. Perhaps I understand now better than they will, but

I can't simply wave my magic wand and make it all come right. You came here this morning with some vague idea that you'd only have to tell me about it and it would all turn out to be like it was before you were married. Trust Chris to get me out of it. Isn't that it? Well I'm sorry, Vic, but it just can't be done. It's a bit too big for that.

VIC shrugs. He doesn't know what to say.

2 VIC. Where's David?

3 CHRIS. In the bathroom. I shall have to be getting the breakfast or he'll be late and so will I. And I suppose you could do with something if you've been out all night.

4 VIC. I don't want much.

A pause, during which CHRIS regards him.

5 CHRIS. Look, Vic, I know you're unhappy and I do want to help you.

6 VIC. I've had enough, Chris. It's just a cheat, a lousy rotten cheat.

7 CHRIS. Oh, Vic, people talk glibly about being in love. Books and films are full of it. And it *can* happen that way. You can be in love with someone you hardly know—all rapture and starry eyes. But there's a difference between that and loving. You can't *love* a person till you've lived with them and shared experience. You've got to share living before you can find love. Being *in* love doesn't last, you can find love to take its place. Do you know what I mean, Vic?

8 VIC. I know, Chris. But we never had it in the beginning.

9 CHRIS. Well try to find it now. Think of Ingrid. She loves you, or she did, I know. Losing the baby was a terrible thing for her and she needs somebody now to look after her and comfort her and make her see that life can be good again. You could do that for her. Don't give up like this, Vic. Make your marriage work.

10 VIC. I can't go back to that old bitch.

1   CHRIS. She probably wouldn't have you back.

2   VIC. No.

3   CHRIS. Well, it looks as though we've got a lodger for a few nights.

4   VIC. Don't put yourself out for me.

5   CHRIS. There's no use being silly-clever about it, Vic. You won't want to go home just yet, I suppose?

6   VIC. I haven't got a bloody home.

SCENE 10   THE RECORD SHOP

ARTHUR *is standing talking to* VIC.

7   ARTHUR. I thought I'd better call round and see what you were doing.

8   VIC. You've heard then?

9   ARTHUR. Aye, we've heard.

10   VIC. Bad news travels fast.

11   ARTHUR. Our Christine called round this dinner-time and told us.

12   VIC. Oh, did she?

13   ARTHUR. You'd rather we got it from her than somebody on t'street, wouldn't you?

14   VIC. I suppose so.

15   ARTHUR. Seeing as how you weren't coming to tell us yourself.

16   VIC. Am I welcome, then?

17   ARTHUR. Well, your mother's a bit upset about it.

18   VIC. Aye, well I don't want any rows or arguments about it so I thought I'd steer clear.

19   ARTHUR. She says she doesn't want to see you till you're back with Ingrid again.

20   VIC. Happen she'll have a long time to wait, then.

21   ARTHUR. If that's the way the land lies ...

77

1   VIC. It is. I can be as bloody-minded as anybody else.

2   ARTHUR. It seems to be you've only—

3   VIC. Only meself to blame? So I keep hearing. Well, I've
    told you. I don't want any rows or arguments. I've
    had a bellyful.

4   ARTHUR. You just can't get on wi' yon' woman, is that it?

5   VIC. It's part of it.

6   ARTHUR. D'you think you'd have been all right on your own
    with Ingrid?

7   VIC. How do I know? I've never had the chance.

8   ARTHUR. Our Chris said summat about finding you a flat.
    It seems some teacher friends of David's are going
    abroad or summat and they want somebody to take it
    on for a couple of years. It sounded all right.

9   VIC. Oh?

10   ARTHUR. You'd be better then, wouldn't you?

11   VIC. I don't know that Ingrid 'ud come now.

12   ARTHUR. Well, you'll have to bloody make her, won't you?

13   VIC. That's all very well, but—

14   ARTHUR. Show some spirit, man. Lay the law down. And
    get shut o' that silly woman. I could see trouble with
    her from the start.

15   VIC. So could I, but it didn't help much.

16   ARTHUR. Look, I shall have to be off. I'm on me way to
    t'doctor's. If I don't get there soon I shan't be away afore
    midnight.

17   VIC. What's wrong?

18   ARTHUR. Oh, it's nowt much. Just a funny twinge in me
    back. I'm going to pacify your mother more than owt
    else. I'll call in in a day or two and see how you're
    doing.

19   VIC. Suit yourself.

20   ARTHUR. Now look here, it seems to me you've got yourself
    across with enough folk without starting it with me.

21   VIC. I'm sorry, Dad. I'm just touchy, I suppose.

1 ARTHUR. Well think about it, and think hard. I'll be seeing you.

2 VIC. Aye, all right. So long. And thanks. [ARTHUR *goes out.* VIC *looks at his watch and locks the door. As he turns away somebody tries the handle then raps on the glass.*] We're closed. Can't you read? [*The tapping is heard again and* VIC *opens the door.*] We're shut.

3 MR. ROTHWELL. I can see that.

4 VIC. Oh, it's you. [*He lets* MR. ROTHWELL *in.*] Looks like Father's Day. I've just had me dad in.

5 MR. ROTHWELL. I thought I saw him going away.

6 VIC. I don't know what you've come for but I've just been telling him—I don't want any rows or arguments.

7 MR. ROTHWELL. I've come to talk to you, not have a row.

8 VIC. Oh.

9 MR. ROTHWELL. It's a mess.

10 VIC. Yes.

11 MR. ROTHWELL. Have you finished here now?

12 VIC. Yes. I was just going.

13 MR. ROTHWELL. Would you like to walk round the corner and talk over a drink?

14 VIC. If I start drinking now I'll be dopy all evening.

15 MR. ROTHWELL. Just as you like. You're not much of a drinker, are you?

16 VIC. No, I get drunk pretty easily, really.

17 MR. ROTHWELL. I've a good mind to send you a cleaning bill for the carpet.

18 VIC. I'm sorry about that. I was pretty sozzled but that was an accident.

19 MR. ROTHWELL. I gather the beer loosened your tongue a bit as well.

20 VIC. I said a few things.

21 MR. ROTHWELL. Perhaps you had some cause to fly off the handle; I don't know.

22 VIC. You've only heard one side of it.

1   MR. ROTHWELL. Like to tell me yours?

2   VIC. I don't see how I can, really.

3   MR. ROTHWELL. You mean without offending me. Well try.

> *This is awkward for* VIC. *He cannot be as frank about his feelings for* INGRID *as he was with* CHRIS, *and so he is forced to concentrate on* MRS. ROTHWELL's *part in the break-up.*

4   VIC. Well, I know you meant well offering us a place but I just don't think Ingrid's mother liked me from the start, and she's never really given us a chance. I don't know if you know it but she influences Ingrid a lot.

5   MR. ROTHWELL. I know. That's partly because I'm away so much.

6   VIC. Well, it got so Ingrid was listening to her mother all the time. I felt like a lodger, only she was always telling me what responsibilities I'd got. But I never had a chance to take responsibility. Then when the accident happened and Ingrid lost the baby and she never let me know, I was so wild I nearly walked out there and then.

7   MR. ROTHWELL. What do you mean, she didn't let you know?

8   VIC. She never rang me. Mrs. Oliphant came into the shop hours later and told me. Then she acted as if I'd pushed Ingrid down the stairs.

9   MR. ROTHWELL. I see. Anyway, you decided to stay.

10   VIC. Yes. And things just got worse. Ingrid didn't seem to have any life in her any more and I couldn't snap her out of it. She said I'd no consideration.

11   MR. ROTHWELL. It was a big shock for her, you know.

12   VIC. It must have been. But I got the feeling her mother was encouraging her not to get better.

13   MR. ROTHWELL. By and large, then, you'd say that Ingrid's mother was at the bottom of the trouble?

14   VIC. Well, yes . . . I would.

15   MR. ROTHWELL. But still, I get the impression that you've felt badly done to for some time. Almost as though

marriage itself had been imposed on you. Do you wish you'd never got married?

2 VIC. Yes, I do.

3 MR. ROTHWELL. Why did you get married? Because you wanted Ingrid or because of the baby? [*no reply*] All right, then: do you want to stay married to Ingrid?

4 VIC. I won't be married to her and her mother.

5 MR. ROTHWELL. That's not unreasonable. But you've nowhere to take a wife, nothing to offer her. You're in a pretty poor position.

6 VIC. Oh, it's not all that bad from where I'm standing. I walked out and I can stay out. There's no baby to think about now, and nobody's going to push me into anything.

7 MR. ROTHWELL. Who's pushing?

8 VIC. I just don't want everybody thinking I'm hanging about waiting for Ingrid to take me back. I did the walking out, remember?

9 MR. ROTHWELL. That's true. And anyway, you don't know that Ingrid wants you now, do you?

10 VIC. She hadn't shown much sign of it for a bit.

11 MR. ROTHWELL. Well then, perhaps it'll be best to call it a day. Six months isn't long. You'll both get over it. You wouldn't object to Ingrid asking for a divorce, would you?

12 VIC. What grounds has she?

13 MR. ROTHWELL. I don't know. Desertion, perhaps. She's young and attractive and she'll want to get married again. So will you, perhaps.

14 VIC. I've had a bellyful of being married.

15 MR. ROTHWELL. So now you're going to chuck it and get out.

16 VIC. I haven't said that.

17 MR. ROTHWELL. I thought you had.

18 VIC. I only said I could if I wanted to. I'm not waiting around for any favours and I'm not going to be pushed

into anything. You can tell Ingrid that from me, and her mother.

2   MR. ROTHWELL. I'm not carrying any messages, Vic. If you want to say anything to Ingrid you'll have to tell her yourself.

3   VIC. A fat chance I've got of telling her anything with her mother on guard. She doesn't like me, y'know.

4   MR. ROTHWELL. I know she doesn't. But I like you, and I don't shy from the idea of you being my son-in-law.

5   VIC. Thanks very much.

MR. ROTHWELL picks up a transistor radio and looks at it.

6   MR. ROTHWELL. Are these any good?

7   VIC. They're all right for the money.

8   MR. ROTHWELL. Mmm . . . so where do we go from here?

9   VIC. Suppose I said I'd got the chance of a flat?

10 MR. ROTHWELL. I'd say it made things more promising. If you make a home for Ingrid and she refuses to come to you then you're the injured party, legally.

11 VIC. Do you think she would come? She'd have to go out to work again to help buy the furniture and pay the rent.

12 MR. ROTHWELL. Why don't you ask her?

13 VIC. How the hell can I? Her mother 'ud go hairless at the thought.

14 MR. ROTHWELL. I don't want a bald wife, but we shall have to risk that, shan't we?

The lights fade.

SCENE 11   THE PARK
            Night

VIC *and* INGRID *stroll on from side.*

15 VIC. Here we are, then. Back where we started from.

1　INGRID. How far do you think we've walked?

2　VIC. Feels like ten miles.

3　INGRID. Mmm. I've enjoyed it, though.

4　VIC. It's nice to be able to talk and say what you want to say without thinking about somebody in the next room.

5　INGRID. Do you realize how long it is since we had a proper talk about anything?

6　VIC. Ages ... And it's not something you can sort out all in a minute. I've been thinking about it for days, trying to decide what's best.

7　INGRID. Me too. Oh, I'm glad the trouble's over and it's going to be all right.

8　VIC. You know you're going to have to stand up to her, don't you?

9　INGRID. Yes, I know.

10　VIC. You'll have to make her see you've made your mind up and you can't be talked out of it.

11　INGRID. It won't be easy. She's dead set against you now.

12　VIC. Your dad's with us, anyway.

13　INGRID. He's a brick, is me dad. I don't know what we'd have done without him.

14　VIC. Aye, he's a right nice feller. I like him.

15　INGRID. Vic, when do you think we can look at the flat?

16　VIC. Sooner the better. They'll be expecting us any time.

17　INGRID. You do want to take it, don't you, Vic?

18　VIC. Beggars can't be choosers, can they? It's a bit steep but we'll manage, I suppose.

19　INGRID. No, what I mean is ... you want to take it so's we can be together.

20　VIC [thoughtfully]. I reckon we haven't had a fair try. We're married and we ought to see how it works out with just the two of us. P'raps we'll be chucking the pots at each other in a couple of months, but at least we shan't be able to blame anybody else.

1   INGRID. I don't think we shall ... We've had a rotten six months, haven't we?

2   VIC. I'll say. If anybody had told me a year ago all that was going to happen I'd never have believed them.

3   INGRID. You know, Vic, all that time when I didn't want you to make love to me. Well it wasn't that I didn't want you to really. Only it just didn't seem right somehow when we were at home.

4   VIC. I think I know what you mean. You know you're a different person as soon as you get out of that house.

5   INGRID. It'll be all right when we're on our own.

6   VIC. I hope so.

7   INGRID. It will, Vic. I promise.

8   VIC [*embracing her*]. The trouble is waiting.

9   INGRID. It won't be long.

10   VIC. There's no time like the present.

11   INGRID [*laughing*]. Oh, Vic ... Suppose somebody comes?

12   VIC. Nobody ever did before. And besides, we *are* married.

13   INGRID. You're the last person they'd think I was married to.

14   VIC. I suppose so.

They kiss.

15   INGRID. Oh, Vic, we'll make it work. We'll find a kind of loving to carry us through.

16   VIC. We'd better, love. It's for a long, long time.

17   INGRID. We will. I know we will.

18   VIC. You know, I've been thinking about all this and I reckon it's taught me something. I mean, people talk about sin and punishment and all that, but I think there's no such thing. I think there's what you do and what comes of it. If you do wrong things, wrong things happen to you. But it doesn't stop there because there's a chance. After everything else there's always chance and when you do your best you can't allow for that. What it boils down to is you've got to do your best,

what you think's right. You do your best and hope for the same. That's what everybody's doing all over the world. And if you do your best and still get a rotten deal, well you can't complain because that's life. You might say you don't deserve it, but that's just your story.

2   INGRID. You're a funny lad, Vic.

3   VIC. Am I?

4   INGRID. Yes. And I love you.

5   VIC. Well, that's all right, then. [*They kiss and* INGRID *suddenly shivers.*] Are you cold?

6   INGRID. I didn't feel it while we were walking.

7   VIC. We'd better go. There's another day tomorrow. [*He takes her arm and as they begin to stroll off he looks up at the sky.*] Do you realize it'll be Christmas again in a fortnight?

CURTAIN

Notes and Questions

NOVEL INTO PLAY

ALFRED BRADLEY

Somebody told me about *A Kind of Loving* before it was published. I got hold of an advance copy, read it at a sitting, and was so excited by the quality of the writing that I read it again almost at once. It appealed to me because, although it was about an ordinary young couple in a rather dull provincial town, it explored the problems that face people everywhere. Most of us are attracted to members of the opposite sex, and most of us fall in love at least once in a lifetime: it isn't always easy to separate one from the other before it is too late. If you look at the young married couples you know, you will probably feel that there are many who, like Vic and Ingrid, have settled for something less than love: Stan Barstow has captured the relationship between one young couple so exactly that the story has a wider, universal significance.

Willis Hall and Keith Waterhouse wrote an excellent screenplay for the film of the novel, which has been seen by millions of people, but I was delighted when the author invited me to work on the stage adaptation, as this gives an opportunity for different actors and directors to interpret the story afresh, and perhaps to bring out rather different sides of the original. Having decided that it was worthwhile to adapt the novel for the theatre, we found that it presented difficulties as the original story is told in the first person. In our first draft we put in speeches addressed directly to the audience. This meant that Vic could step out of the picture frame and explain how he *felt* at particular moments; but in production the device seemed clumsy and we decided to rewrite the play making Willy a more sympathetic character than he is in the novel, so that Vic was able to tell the audience what he felt by confiding in him. This did not solve all the problems however; for example, Vic's feelings about Ingrid, which change gradually in the novel, had to be expressed in the short scene in the park where she gives him the extravagant birthday present (page 35). In a case like this a great deal depends on the producer

89

of the play being able to point out the significance behind each line of dialogue so that the actors can show us what is going on inside the characters: the things they *don't* say are sometimes more important than the ones they do.

As well as the obvious need to reduce a full-length novel into a play lasting not much more than two hours by removing almost everything which is not strictly relevant to the main theme, there are physical limitations to the number of naturalistic settings which can be put on to a stage. One of the first practical tasks is to bring these down to a workable number. In the *film* version, the fact that Vic had a part-time job in the record shop was played down and seemed unimportant. In our stage adaptation his work in the record shop is essential: firstly it is a way of establishing that (unlike Ingrid) Vic wanted to extend his experience of the world around him and was anxious to learn; secondly it provided a place where characters as varied as Mrs. Oliphant, Willy, Mr. Brown and Mr. Rothwell could meet naturally. I stress naturally, because this is a realistic play, and if the belief of the audience is stretched too far they will cease to believe in the central characters and lose interest in the story. An example comes just before the end of the play: we wanted to show how the two fathers reacted to the break-up of the marriage and also to convey certain information which was essential to the plot. It was easy enough to bring Mr. Brown to the record shop so that he could tell Vic about the offer of the flat, but it seemed unlikely that Mr. Rothwell would arrive at exactly the same time and even more of a coincidence that there should be a moment when there were no other customers in the shop. In the end the problem was resolved by setting the scene at the end of the day, as the shop was about to close. It seemed reasonable that then Mr. Brown might drop in on his way to the Doctor, and credible that a sensitive man like Mr. Rothwell would call as he would expect Vic to be alone. Vic's line 'It looks like Father's day' points out the coincidence to the audience before they can start to think how unlikely it is, and incidentally shows that Vic still has a quick sense of humour which helps him to keep our sympathy. This is just one example of the thinking which has to go into the construction of a scene, and how *practical* problems of staging are closely connected with our *ideas* about the characters. A comparison with the novel will show how we avoided the necessity of building a pub, a teashop, a cinema, and of bringing a bus on stage!

After discussion about the various ways of staging the play, Colin George, who directed the first production at the Sheffield Playhouse, worked out an ingenious composite setting (see pages 93–5). These allowed Vic (who hardly leaves the stage right through the play) to walk down a few steps from the park bench into the Browns' living-room or the drawing office in the first half of the play and the Rothwells' house and the record shop in the second. By using lighting to show up and emphasize different parts of the set for different scenes the action was able to move easily from one location to another, without any breaks between scenes.

Putting on a play is an activity which involves a group of people, and the writer has to be willing to listen to suggestions which may come from the actors, director or designer. Having been invited to attend rehearsals, we were able to clarify important points of plot, cut scenes or extend dialogue to cover essential action or to pare it down when it became obvious that the intelligence that a good actor brings to a part may make three or four spoken words do the work of a paragraph. The script as you read it now was not finalized until the actors and director had breathed life into it.

Usually a novelist gets very little reaction from his readers, apart from those who are paid to review his work when it is first published, so it is not surprising that Stan Barstow finds it stimulating to work in the theatre where he can see at first hand how his characters affect an audience. The subtleties of a novel are sometimes lost and a smile easily turns into a gale of laughter when it is experienced by many people at the same time: is there any point then in turning a novel like *A Kind of Loving* into a stage play? You must judge for yourself, but the productions that we have seen so far, which have played to predominantly young audiences, suggest that there is.

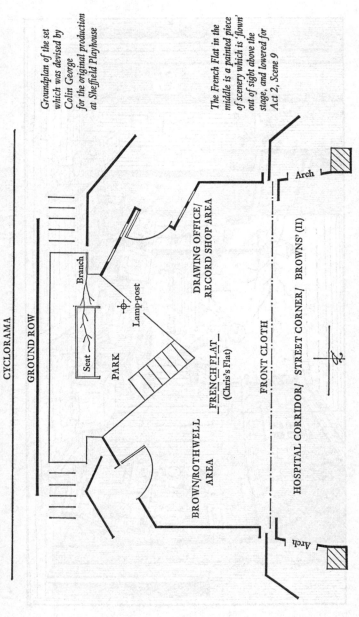

CYCLORAMA

GROUND ROW

Groundplan of the set which was devised by Colin George for the original production at Sheffield Playhouse

The French Flat in the middle is a painted piece of scenery which is 'flown' out of sight above the stage, and lowered for Act 2, Scene 9

Branch

Seat

Lamp-post

PARK

FRENCH FLAT
(Chris's Flat)

DRAWING OFFICE/
RECORD SHOP AREA

Arch

BROWN/ROTHWELL
AREA

FRONT CLOTH

HOSPITAL CORRIDOR/ STREET CORNER/ BROWNS' (II)

Arch

Composite set (Sheffield Playhouse) of the Browns' living-room, the park and the drawing office.

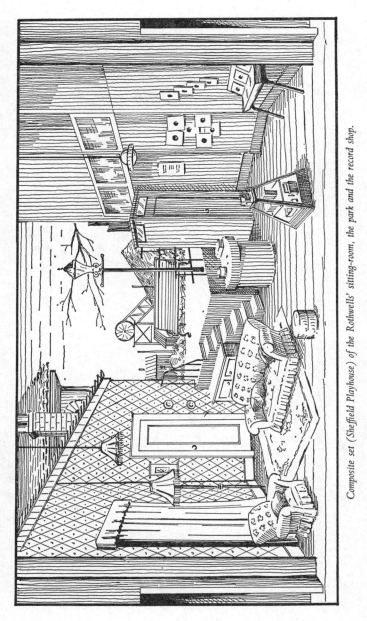

Composite set (Sheffield Playhouse) of the Rothwells' sitting-room, the park and the record shop.

95

THE AUTHORS

Stan Barstow was born in 1928, the only child of a coal miner, in the West Riding of Yorkshire, where he still lives with his wife and two children. After he had been to Ossett Grammar School, he began his working life, like Vic in *A Kind of Loving*, in the drawing office of a local engineering firm. Like Vic he began to feel frustrated in this job, and it was then that he developed his interest in writing. The success of his first novel, *A Kind of Loving*, which was a Book Society Choice in 1960, and the notable film subsequently made from it, allowed him to take up writing full-time in 1962. *The Desperadoes*, a collection of short stories, was published in 1961. Many of the stories were first broadcast by the BBC and the author himself has recorded two of them: *One of the Virtues* and *The Human Element* (Longman LG582 233763). Four novels followed: *Ask me Tomorrow, Joby, The Watchers on the Shore*, and *A Raging Calm* in 1962, 1964, 1966 and 1968. He has also edited a volume of writing about childhood, *Through the Green Wood*.

His interests include music and the cinema, and he has written for radio, television, and the theatre, contributed to newspapers and magazines, and made a number of radio and television appearances.

Alfred Bradley has collaborated with Stan Barstow, whom he knows well, a number of times, producing him as a reader and directing radio versions of his stories on BBC.

OTHER BOOKS BY STAN BARSTOW

These books are especially recommended to readers of this play:

A Kind of Loving (the novel on which this play is based), Michael Joseph, or Hutchinson's *Unicorn Books*.

The Watchers on the Shore (a sequel to this story of Vic and Ingrid), Michael Joseph.

Ask Me Tomorrow, Michael Joseph or Penguin.

Joby, Bodley Head Series.

The Human Element and other Stories, Longman Imprint Books.

A Raging Calm, Michael Joseph.

QUESTIONS FOR DISCUSSION

1. What picture of the Browns' family life do you get from the first scene? Does Arthur have any especially likeable characteristics? Does he seem to have any weaknesses?

2. How does Vic compare with the other young men working at Dawson Whittaker's in his interests, his attitude to the job, and his general manner?

3. In *Act 1 scenes 4,6* and *8* we see three of the early occasions on which Ingrid and Vic go out together. Are there any signs to show whether they are well suited to each other, or whether they have unfortunate differences?

4. What does Ingrid mean when she says to Vic (*page 44, speech 7*) 'That's the trouble, isn't it? I mean we couldn't tell anybody how it is.'?

5. Do you believe Vic when he tries to explain his feelings to Ingrid?
   'I don't know how I do feel half the time. Sometimes I feel rotten about it all and then I think it's not fair to either of us to carry on . . . I did try to break it off, y'know, when I found out it wasn't the same as I'd thought.' (*page 46, speech 4*)

6. Is Vic's attitude in the scene where they discuss Ingrid's pregnancy (*Act 1, scene 15*) what you would have expected from what the play has shown of him so far?

7. What similarities and what differences do you find in the two families (Vic's and Ingrid's) in the scenes in which Vic breaks the news to his parents (*Act 2, scene 1*) and meets hers for the first time (*Act 2, scene 1*)?

8. 'There's no bloody perhaps about it.' (*page 64, speech 15*) This is Vic's answer by the end of the scene in which Ingrid refuses to go to the concert. What has led him to feel like this?

9. When Vic turns up at his sister's flat hoping for sympathy (*Act 2, scene 9*), she unexpectedly makes him (and us)

look at the situation in a new light. To what extent do you agree with her point of view?

10   In the film version of *A Kind of Loving*, the character of Mr. Van Huyten was cut out. Would this cut lose any important ideas in the story?

11   The play ends with the hope for the future:
> 'Oh, Vic, we'll make it work. We'll find a kind of loving to carry us through.'
> 'We'd better, love. It's for a long, long time.' (*page 84 speeches 15 and 16*).

From all you've seen of the play, what is your estimate of their chances of 'making it work'?